The Hound
of
The Baskervilles

Dramatised by
Claire Malcomson

Paperback ISBN 9781780925103
ePub ISBN 9781780925110
PDF ISBN 9781780925127

Published in the UK by MX Publishing
335 Princess Park Manor, Royal Drive,
London, N11 3GX
www.mxpublishing.co.uk

Cover design by www.staunch.com

To contact Claire about performance rights etc please
email: clairemalcomson@hotmail.co.uk

THE HOUND OF THE BASKERVILLES adapted by Claire Malcomson

The play can be acted with 7-9 plus actors, with actors doubling.

First produced at Hever Castle and The Mill at Guildford's Yvonne Arnaud in May 2013.

Sherlock Holmes	Peter Wicks
Dr John Watson	John Conway
Sir Henry Baskerville	Daniel Moore
Dr Jane Mortimer	Claire Dyson
Barrymore	Graham Christopher
Mrs Barrymore	Victoria Durrant
Jack Stapleton	Simon Chappell
Maria Stapleton	Andrea Nodroum
Laura Lyons	Claire Malcomson
Maiden/Post Mistress	Laurie Elcoate May
Seldon/Yokel Sir Hugo	Clayton Wellman
Yokel/Post mistress	Stacey Roberts
Washer Woman Yokel	Kate Hefferman

The Play directed by Claire Malcomson

The action takes place at Sherlock Holmes' accommodation in Baker Street, Baskerville Hall and on Dartmoor.

Date 1906

Cast List:-

Sherlock Holmes	Famous Detective
Dr John Watson	His Trusty Right Hand Man
Dr Jane Mortimer	Local GP
Sir Henry Baskerville	Heir to Baskerville Hall
Barrymore	Butler
Mrs Barrymore	House Keeper
Jack Stapleton	Close Neighbour to the Hall
Maria Stapleton	Close Neighbour to the Hall
Laura Lyons	Daughter of Local Neighbour
Selden	Escaped Prisoner
Postmistress/master	Post Office and Shop Keeper
Various Yokels and Village Folk	

Most of the play is on the stage, with the use of the extreme right and left for smaller scenes. The Moor is around the audience and on the main stage, depending on the set up of the theatre and auditorium.

PROLOGUE

<u>Watson</u> **Phantom dogs are a favourite in British myths and folk stories and are often referred to as 'Black Dogs'. Throughout the kingdom public houses and lanes are named after them, 'The Old Black Dog' or 'Black Dog Lane'. The stories are usually about rather benign animals which are supposed to appear when something horrific has happened to their owners. The fable of the Phantom Boar Hound of Wales and, to this day, the famous Surrey Puma is still reputed to roam the North Downs. These spectral creatures are said to be luminous, with saucer like eyes, and even have flames coming from their mouths. They appear from nowhere and can attack without warning. Create with me now, as we travel swiftly though time from London to Dartmoor, all the scenes of the mystery; one moment here, one moment there, and learn of the most infamous creature of all - 'The Hound of the Baskervilles'. Does it really exist or is it too a myth? Or are these fears all coming from our own vivid imaginations?**

Act 1 Scene 1 Holmes' Office

Watson	To J. Mortimer, from your friends of the C.C.H 1891 *(Looking at walking stick.)*
Holmes	Well, Watson, what do you make of it? *(Back to Watson.)*
Watson	How did you know what I was doing? I believe you have eyes in the back of your head.
Holmes	Tell me, Watson, what do you make of our visitor's stick? Since we have been so unfortunate as to have missed him and have no notion of his errand, this accidental souvenir becomes of importance. Let me hear you reconstruct the person by an examination of it.
Watson	I think *(to the audience)* following as far as I could the methods of my companion, *(to Holmes)* that Mortimer is a successful, elderly medical man, well-esteemed since those who know him gave him this mark of their appreciation.
Holmes.	Good Watson. Excellent!
Watson	I think also that the probability is in favour of his being a country practitioner whom does a great deal of his visiting on foot.
Holmes	Why so?
Watson	Because this stick, though originally a very handsome one has been so knocked about that I can hardly imagine a town practitioner carrying it. The thick-iron ferrule is worn down, so it is evident that he has done a great amount of walking with it.
Holmes	Perfectly sound!
Watson	There is the 'friends of the C.C.H.' I should guess that to be the 'Something Hunt', the local hunt to whose members he has probably given some medical assistance, and which has made him a small presentation in return.
Holmes	Really, Watson, you excel yourself. It may be that you are not yourself luminous, but you are a conductor of light. Some people without possessing genius have a remarkable power of stimulating it. I confess, my dear fellow, that I am very much in your debt. (Inspects stick.) Interesting, though elementary. There are certainly one or two indications upon the stick. It gives us the basis for several deductions.
Watson	Has anything escaped me? *(Self-importantly.)* I trust that there is nothing of consequence which I have overlooked?

Holmes	I am afraid, my dear Watson, that most of your conclusions were erroneous. When I said that you stimulated me I meant, to be frank, that in noting your fallacies I was occasionally guided towards the truth. Not that you are entirely wrong in this instance. The person is certainly a country practitioner, and walks a good deal.
Watson	Then I was right!
Holmes	To that extent.
Watson	But that was all?
Holmes	No, no, my dear Watson, not all - by no means all. I would suggest, for example, that a presentation to a doctor is more likely to come from a hospital than from a hunt, and that when the initials 'C.C.' are placed before that hospital the words 'Charing Cross' very naturally suggest themselves.
Watson	You may be right. Well, then, supposing that 'C.C.H.' does stand for 'Charing Cross Hospital,' what further inferences may we draw?
Holmes	Do none suggest themselves? You know my methods. Apply them!
Watson	I can only come to the obvious conclusion that the man has practised in town before going to the country.
Holmes	And this stick was presented the day he left. Now, you will observe that he could not have been on the staff of the hospital, since only a man well-established in a London practice could hold such a position, and such a one would not drift into the country. He could only have been a house-physician; little more than a senior student. And he left ten years ago. The date is on the stick. So your grave, elderly family practitioner vanishes into thin air, my dear Watson, and there emerges a young middle-aged, un-ambitious, absent-minded female, and the possessor of a favourite dog, which I should describe roughly as being large.
Watson	A woman?
Holmes	Can you not smell the scent on the handle?
Watson	*(Laughing.)* You confound me Holmes... Well, at least it is not difficult to find out a few particulars about the woman's age and professional career. *(Takes book from shelf.)* There can be only one who could be our visitor. "Mortimer, Jane, 1891, Grimpen, Dartmoor, Devonshire. House-physician, from 1889 to 1891, at Charing Cross Hospital. Writer of 'Do We Progress?' (Journal of Psychology, March, 1893). Medical Officer for the parishes of Grimpen, Thorsley, and High Barrow."
Holmes	No mention of that local hunt, Watson, but a country doctor, as you very astutely observed. I think that I am fairly justified in my inferences. As to the

adjectives, I said, if I remember right, un-ambitious, and absent-minded. It is my experience that only an un-ambitious one would abandon a London career for the country, and only an absent-minded one who leaves her stick and not her visiting-card after waiting an hour in your room.

Watson   And the dog?

Holmes   Has been in the habit of carrying this stick behind his mistress. The marks of his teeth are very plainly visible. The dog's jaw is so broad it could only be a Mastiff or St Bernard. *(Listens.)* Hush, now is the dramatic moment of fate, Watson, when you hear a step upon the stair which is walking into your life, and you know not whether for good or ill. What does Dr. Jane Mortimer, ask of Sherlock Holmes, the specialist in crime? Come in!

Mortimer   I am so very glad, I was not sure whether I had left it here or in the Shipping Office. I would not lose that stick for the world.

Holmes   A presentation, I see.

Mortimer   Yes, sir.

Holmes   From Charing Cross Hospital

Mortimer   From one or two friends there on the occasion of my marriage.

Holmes   Dear, dear, that's bad.

Mortimer   Why was it bad?

Holmes   Only that you have disarranged our little deductions. Your marriage, you say?

Mortimer   Yes, sir. I married, and so left the hospital, and with it all hopes of a consulting practice. It was necessary to make a home of my own.

Holmes   Come, come, we are not so far wrong, after all. How can I help?

Mortimer   I'm a dabbler in science, Mr. Holmes, a picker up of shells on the shores of the great unknown ocean. I presume that it is Mr. Sherlock Holmes whom I am addressing?

Holmes   No, this is my friend Dr. Watson.

Mortimer   Glad to meet you, sir. I have heard your name mentioned in connection with that of your friend. You interest me very much, Mr. Holmes. I had hardly expected so dolichocephalic a skull or such well-marked supra-orbital development. A cast of your skull, sir, until the original is available, would be an ornament to any anthropological museum.

Holmes	You are an enthusiast in your line of thought, I perceive, Madam, as I am in mine. I presume that it was not merely for the purpose of examining my skull that you have done me the honour to call here last night and again to-day?
Mortimer	No, sir, no, though I am happy to have had the opportunity of doing that as well.
Holmes	I think, Mrs... Dr. Mortimer, you would do wisely if without more ado you would kindly tell me plainly what the exact nature of the problem is in which you demand my assistance.
Mortimer	I have here an old manuscript.
Holmes	Early eighteenth century, unless it is a forgery.
Mortimer	The exact date is 1742. This family paper was committed to my care by Sir Charles Baskerville, whose sudden and tragic death some five months ago created so much excitement in Devonshire. I may say that I was his personal friend as well as his medical attendant. He was a strong-minded man, sir, shrewd, practical, and as unimaginative as I am myself. Yet he took this document very seriously, and his mind was prepared for just such an end as did eventually overtake him. It is a statement of a certain legend which runs in the Baskerville family. The manuscript is short and is intimately connected with the affair. Please take some time to read it.

(Holmes leans back in his chair, placed his finger-tips together, and reads.)

Holmes	Well?
Mortimer	Do you not find it interesting?
Holmes	To a collector of fairy tales.
Mortimer	*(Jane Mortimer draws a folded newspaper out of her pocket.)* Now, Mr. Holmes, this is the Devon County Chronicle of May 14th of this year. It is a short account of the facts elicited at the death of Sir Charles Baskerville which occurred a few days before that date. *(Reads aloud.)*

"The circumstances connected with the death of Sir Charles cannot be said to have been entirely cleared up by the inquest, but at least enough has been done to dispose of those rumours to which local superstition has given rise. There is no reason whatever to suspect foul play, or to imagine that death could be from any but natural causes. Sir Charles was a widower. In spite of his considerable wealth he had simple personal tastes, and his indoor servants at Baskerville Hall consisted of a married couple named Barrymore, the husband acting as butler and the wife as housekeeper. Sir Charles's health had for some time been impaired, and pointed to a weak heart, he was often breathless, and had acute attacks of nervous depression.

The evidence of the Barrymores shows that Sir Charles was in the habit of walking along Yew Alley of Baskerville Hall. On the fourth of May Barrymore prepared Sir Charles luggage as he intended to go to London the next day. That night he went out as usual for his nocturnal walk, on which he was in the habit of smoking a cigar. He never returned. At twelve o'clock

Barrymore, finding the hall door still open, became alarmed, and, lighting a lantern, went in search of his master. The day had been wet, and Sir Charles's footmarks were easily traced down the alley. Halfway down this walk there is a gate which leads out on to the moor. There were indications that Sir Charles had stood for some little time here. He then proceeded down the alley, and it was at the far end of it that his body was discovered.

Barrymore reported that his master's footprints altered their character from the time that he passed the moor-gate, and that he appeared to start walking upon his toes. No signs of violence were to be discovered upon Sir Charles's person, but the post-mortem examination showed long-standing organic disease. This was received positively by the local people as they wish Sir Charles's heir to settle at the Hall without fear of the so called curse. It is understood that the next of kin is Mr. Henry Baskerville, if he be still alive, the son of Sir Charles Baskerville's younger brother. The young man when last heard of was in America."

Mortimer	Those are the public facts, Mr. Holmes, in connection with the death of Sir Charles Baskerville.
Holmes	I must thank you, for calling my attention to a case which certainly presents some features of interest. This article, you say, contains all the public facts?
Mortimer	It does.
Holmes	Then let me have the private ones.
Mortimer	*(Emotionally.)* I have not confided this to anyone. My motive for withholding it from the coroner's inquiry is that I did not want to be seen to be adding to popular superstition. I had the further motive that Baskerville Hall, as the paper hints at, would certainly remain untenanted if anything were done to increase its already rather grim reputation. For both these reasons I thought that I was justified in telling rather less than I knew.

I saw a good deal of Sir Charles Baskerville as not many people live on the moor. With the exception of Mr. Frankland, of Lafter Hall, and Mr. Stapleton, the naturalist, and his sister, no-one lives close by. I met Sir Charles on a professional basis, but he became my husband's and my friend. My husband was a great deal older than I, he passed away 2 years ago. Sir Charles' nervous system was strained to the breaking point. He had taken this legend to heart - so much so that, nothing would induce him to go out upon the moor at night. He was honestly convinced that a dreadful fate overhung his family. The idea of some ghastly presence constantly haunted him.

On my arrival one evening outside the hall, I saw his eyes stare past me with an expression of the most dreadful horror. I caught a glimpse of something which I took to be a large black calf passing at the head of the drive. We checked the spot and found nothing. I stayed with him all that evening. I was convinced that the matter was entirely trivial and that his excitement had no justification. I advised Sir Charles to go to London to relax. His heart was, I knew, affected. Mr. Stapleton, a mutual friend, was also concerned about his state of health.

On the night of Sir Charles's death Barrymore the butler who made the discovery sent for me. I was able to reach Baskerville Hall within an hour of the event. I checked and corroborated all the facts which were mentioned at the inquest. Sir Charles lay on his face, his arms out, his fingers dug into the ground, and his features convulsed with some strong emotion. All that is in the newspaper article is correct except one false statement was made by Barrymore at the inquest. He said that there were no traces upon the ground round the body. He did not observe any. But I did; some little distance off, but fresh and clear.

Watson   Footprints?

Mortimer   Footprints.

Holmes   A man or a woman's?

Mortimer   Mr. Holmes, they were the footprints of a gigantic hound!

Holmes   You saw this? *(Excited.)*

Mortimer   As clearly as I see you.

Holmes   And you said nothing?

Mortimer   What was the use?

Watson   How was it that no one else saw it?

Mortimer   The marks were some twenty yards from the body and no one gave them a thought. I don't suppose I should have done so had I not known about his anxiety about the legend.

Holmes   There are many sheep-dogs on the moor?

Mortimer   No doubt, but this was no sheep-dog.

Holmes   You say it was large?

Mortimer   Enormous.

Holmes   But it had not approached the body?

Mortimer   No.

Holmes   What sort of night was it?

Mortimer   Damp and raw.

Holmes   But not actually raining?

Mortimer   No.

Holmes	What is the alley like?
Mortimer	There are two lines of old yew hedge, twelve feet high and impenetrable. The walk in the centre is about eight feet across.
Holmes	Is there anything between the hedges and the walk?
Mortimer	Yes, there is a strip of grass about six feet broad on either side.
Holmes	The yew hedge is penetrated half-way down by a gate. Is there any other opening?
Mortimer	None.
Holmes	So that to reach the yew alley one either has to come down it from the house or else to enter it by the moor gate?
Mortimer	There is an exit through a summer-house at the far end.
Holmes	Had Sir Charles reached this?
Mortimer	No; he lay about fifty yards from it.
Holmes	Now, tell me, Dr. Mortimer, and this is important, the marks which you saw were on the path and not on the grass?
Mortimer	No marks could show on the grass.
Holmes	Were they on the same side of the path as the moor-gate?
Mortimer	Yes; they were on the edge of the path on the same side as the moor-gate.
Holmes	You interest me exceedingly. Another point ...was the wicket-gate closed?
Mortimer	Closed and padlocked.
Holmes	How high was it?
Mortimer	About four feet high.
Holmes	Then anyone could have got over it?
Mortimer	Yes.
Holmes	And what marks did you see by the wicket-gate?
Mortimer	None in particular.
Holmes	Good heavens! Did no one examine?

Mortimer	Yes, I examined, myself.
Holmes	And found nothing?
Mortimer	It was all very confused. Sir Charles had evidently stood there for five or ten minutes.
Holmes	How do you know that?
Mortimer	Because the ash had twice dropped from his cigar.
Holmes	Excellent! This is a colleague, Watson, after our own heart. But the marks?
Mortimer	He had left his own marks all over that small patch of gravel. I could discern no others.
Holmes	If I had only been there! It is evidently a case of extraordinary interest, and one which presented immense opportunities to the scientific expert. The gravel, a page upon which I might have read so much, will be smudged by the rain and defaced by the clogs of curious peasants, by now. Oh, Dr. Mortimer, Dr. Mortimer, to think that you should not have called me in! You have indeed much to answer for.
Mortimer	I could not call you in, Mr. Holmes, without disclosing these facts to the world, and I have already given my reasons for not wishing to do so. Besides, besides...
Holmes	Why do you hesitate?
Mortimer	There is a realm in which the most acute and most experienced of detectives is helpless.
Watson	You mean that the thing is supernatural?
Mortimer	I did not positively say so.
Holmes	No, but you evidently think it.
Mortimer	Since the tragedy, Mr. Holmes, I have heard of several incidents which are hard to reconcile with the settled order of Nature.
Holmes	For example?
Mortimer	I've now been told since the terrible event occurred several people had seen a creature upon the moor which corresponds with this Baskerville demon, and which could not possibly be any animal known to science. They all agreed that it was a huge creature, luminous, ghastly, and spectral. I have cross-examined these men, they all tell the same story. I assure you that there is a reign of terror in the district, and that it is a hardy man who will cross the moor at night.

Holmes	And you, a doctor believe it to be supernatural?
Mortimer	I do not know what to believe.
Holmes	Up till now I have confined my investigations to this world. In a modest way I have combated evil, but to take on the Father of Evil himself would, perhaps, be too ambitious a task... However, you must admit that the footmark is material.
Mortimer	The legend says the original hound was material enough to tug a man's throat out, and yet he was diabolical as well.
Holmes	It seems that you agree with the supernaturalists. But if you hold these views why have you come to me? You tell me in the same breath that it is useless to investigate Sir Charles's death, and that you desire me to do it.
Mortimer	I did not say that I desired you to do it.
Holmes	Then, how can I assist you?
Mortimer	By advising me as to what I should do with Sir Henry Baskerville, who arrives at Waterloo Station very soon.
Watson	He being the heir?
Mortimer	Yes. On the death of Sir Charles we found this young gentleman had been farming in Canada. He is known to be an excellent fellow in every way. I speak now as a trustee and executor of Sir Charles's will.
Holmes	There is no other claimant, I presume?
Mortimer	None. Charles was the eldest of three brothers. The second brother, who died young, is the father of this lad Henry. The third, Rodger, was the black sheep of the family. He came of the old masterful Baskerville strain and was the very image, they tell me, of the family picture of old Hugo. He fled to Central America, and died there of yellow fever. Henry is the last of the Baskervilles. Now, Mr. Holmes, what would you advise me to do with him?
Holmes	Why should he not go to the home of his fathers'?
Mortimer	I'm sure that Sir Charles would have warned me against bringing his only heir to that deadly place. But the prosperity of the whole poor, bleak countryside depends on Henry now. All the good work which has been done by Sir Charles will crash to the ground if there is no tenant of the Hall. However, I do not want my interest in the matter to sway my decision, that's why I ask for your advice.
Holmes	But surely, if your supernatural theory be correct, the evil would reach him in London as easily as in Devonshire.

Mortimer	So your advice is that the young man will be as safe in Devonshire as in London? He comes in fifty minutes. What would you recommend?
Holmes	I recommend, that you take an hansom cab and proceed to Waterloo to meet Sir Henry Baskerville.
Mortimer	And then?
Holmes	Say nothing to him at all until I have made up my mind about what to do. It will help if you will bring Sir Henry Baskerville with you, here tomorrow morning at 10.
Mortimer	I will do so, Mr. Holmes.
Holmes	Only one more question, Dr. Mortimer. You say that before Sir Charles Baskerville's death several people saw this apparition upon the moor?
Mortimer	Three people did.
Holmes	Did any see it after?
Mortimer	I have not heard of any.
Holmes	Thank you. Good-morning.
	(Mortimer exits)
Holmes	*(Enjoying the challenge of the mystery.)*...Going out, Watson?
Watson	Unless I can help you?
Holmes	When you pass Bradley's, would you ask him to send up a pound of the strongest shag tobacco? *(Watson nods.)*Thank you. It would be as well if you could make it convenient not to return before evening.
Watson	I shall leave you in peace.
Holmes	And I shall visit Devonshire.
Watson	In Spirit?
Holmes	Exactly. My body will remain in this armchair.
	Same scene – an hour or so later
Watson	*(Looking at a map.)* Based on this, Holmes, it would seem to be a pretty wild place.
Holmes	Yes, the setting is a worthy one for the devil to have a hand.

Watson	So you are inclined to believe the supernatural explanation.
Holmes	The devil's agents may be of flesh and blood, may they not? That change in the footprints. What do you make of that? Why should a man walk on tiptoe down the alley?
Watson	What, then?
Holmes	He was running, Watson - running desperately, running for his life, running until he burst his heart and fell dead upon his face.
Watson	Running, from what?
Holmes	There lies our problem. There are indications that the man was crazed with fear before ever he began to run.
Watson	How can you say that?
Holmes	Only a man who had lost his wits would have run away from the house instead of towards it. He ran with cries for help in the direction where help was least likely to be. Then, again, who was he waiting for that night, and why was he waiting for them in the Yew Alley rather than in his own house?
Watson	You think that he was waiting for someone?
Holmes	The man was elderly and infirm. We can understand his taking an evening stroll, but the night was damp and cold. Why would he stand there for five or ten minutes? As Dr. Mortimer, with more practical sense than I should have given her credit for, deduced from the cigar ash.
Watson	But he went out every evening.
Holmes	The evidence is that he avoided the moor. That night he waited near there. It was the night before he made his departure for London. The thing takes shape, Watson. It becomes coherent. Hand me my violin, all further thought upon this business is postponed until we have had the advantage of meeting Dr. Mortimer and Sir Henry Baskerville in the morning.

--- *Black out*   -----------------------

Scene 2 Holmes' Office

(Holmes in dressing-gown. Clock striking ten when Dr. Mortimer enters, followed by the young baronet. Henry wears a distinctive tweed jacket and has the weather-beaten appearance of one who has spent most of his time in the open air. American/Canadian accent.)

Mortimer   This is Sir Henry Baskerville.

Henry   Why, yes and the strange thing is, Mr. Sherlock Holmes, if my new friend here hadn't brought me here today I would have sought you out myself as I understand that you think out little puzzles, and I've had one this morning which wants more thinking out than I am able to give it.

Holmes   Pray take a seat, Sir Henry.

Mortimer   Henry I'm sure it's only a joke. It was this letter, if you can call it a letter, which arrived this morning. (They all examine the envelope.)

Watson   Sir Henry Baskerville, Northumberland Hotel, Charing Cross with yesterday's date.

Holmes   Who knew that you were going to the Northumberland Hotel?

Henry   No one could have known. We only decided after I met Dr. Mortimer.

Holmes   But Dr. Mortimer was no doubt already stopping there?

Mortimer   No, I had been staying with a friend. There was no possible indication that we intended to go to this hotel.

Holmes   Hum! Someone seems to be very deeply interested in your movements. *(Takes letter out of envelope and reads out.)* ...As you value your life or your reason keep away from the moor. The word "moor" is the only one printed in ink.

Henry   Now, perhaps you will tell me, Mr. Holmes, what in thunder is the meaning of that? And who it is that takes so much interest in my affairs?

Holmes   What do you make of it, Dr. Mortimer? There's certainly nothing supernatural about this, at any rate?

Mortimer   No, sir, but it might very well come from someone who was convinced that the business is supernatural.

Henry   What business? It seems to me that all of you know a great deal more than I do about my own affairs.

Holmes   You shall share our knowledge before you leave this room, Sir Henry. I promise you that. For the moment we will concentrate on this very interesting document, which must have been put together and posted yesterday evening. Have you yesterday's Times, Watson?

Watson	Yes, it's here.
Holmes	Might I trouble you for it -- the inside page, please, with the leading articles? Capital article this on free trade. (Studying newspaper.)
Henry	Hu hum. Aren't we a bit off the trail so far as that note is concerned?
Holmes	On the contrary, I think we are particularly hot upon the trail, Sir Henry. Watson here knows more about my methods than you do, but I fear that even he has not quite grasped the significance.
Watson	No, I confess that I see no connection.
Holmes	And yet, my dear Watson, there is so very close a connection that the one is extracted out of the other. 'You,' 'your,' 'your,' 'life,' 'reason,' 'value,' 'keep away,' 'from the.' Don't you see now where these words have been taken from?
Henry	By thunder, you're right! Well, if that isn't smart!
Holmes	If any possible doubt remained it is settled by the fact that 'keep away' and 'from the' are cut out in one piece.
Henry	Well, now - so it is! Really, Mr. Holmes, this exceeds anything which I could have imagined. I could understand anyone saying that the words were from a newspaper; but that you should name which, and add that it came from the leading article, is really one of the most remarkable things which I have ever known. How did you do it?
Holmes	This is my special hobby, to my eyes the difference between the leaded bourgeois type of a Times article and the slovenly print of an evening half-penny paper are obvious. The detection of types is one of the most elementary branches of knowledge to the special expert in crime. A 'Times' leading article is entirely distinctive, and these words could have been taken from nothing else. As it was done yesterday the strong probability was that we should find the words in yesterday's issue.
Henry	So far as I can follow you, then, Mr. Holmes, someone cut out this message with a pair of scissors –
Holmes	Nail-scissors. You can see that they were very short-bladed scissors, since the cutter had to take two snips over 'keep away.'
Watson	That is so. Someone, then, cut out the message with a pair of short-bladed scissors, applied it to the page with paste –
Holmes	Gum.

Henry	With gum on to the paper. But I want to know why the word 'moor' should have been written.
Holmes	Because he could not find it in print. The other words were all simple and might be found in any issue, but 'moor' would be less common
Mortimer	Why, of course, that would explain it. Have you read anything else in this message, Mr. Holmes?
Holmes	There are one or two indications, and yet the utmost pains have been taken to remove all clues. The address, you observe is printed in rough characters. But The Times is a paper which is seldom found in any hands but those of the highly educated. We may take it, therefore, that the letter was composed by an educated man who wished to pose as an uneducated one, and his effort to conceal his own writing suggests that that writing might be known, or come to be known, by you. Again, you will observe that the words are not gummed on in an accurate line, but that some are much higher than others. 'Life,' for example is quite out of its proper place. That may point to carelessness or it may point to agitation and hurry upon the part of the cutter. On the whole I incline to the latter view, since the matter was evidently important, and it is unlikely that the composer of such a letter would be careless. If he were in a hurry it opens up the interesting question why he should be in a hurry, since any letter posted up to early morning would reach Sir Henry before he would leave his hotel. Did the composer fear an interruption - and from whom?
Mortimer	We are coming now rather into the region of guesswork.
Holmes	More the region where we balance probabilities and choose the most likely. We must always have some material basis on which to start our speculation. Now, you would call it a guess, but I am almost certain that this address has been written in a hotel.
Henry	How in the world can you say that?
Holmes	If you examine it carefully you will see that both the pen and the ink have given the writer trouble. The pen has spluttered twice in a single word and has run dry three times in a short address, showing that there was very little ink in the bottle. Now, a private pen or ink-bottle is seldom allowed to be in such a state, and the combination of the two must be quite rare. But you know the hotel ink and the hotel pen, where it is rare to get anything else. Yes, I have very little hesitation in saying that could we examine the waste-paper baskets of the hotels around Charing Cross until we found the remains of the mutilated Times leader we could lay our hands straight upon the person who sent this singular message. Halloa! Halloa! What's this? *(Holding paper an inch or two from his eyes. He's actually smelling the letter.)*
Watson	Well?
Holmes	Nothing, it is a blank half-sheet of paper, without even a water-mark upon it. I think we have drawn as much as we can from this curious letter; and now, Sir

	Henry, has anything else of interest happened to you since you have been in London?
Henry	Why, no, Mr. Holmes. I think not.
Holmes	You have not observed anyone follow or watch you?
Henry	I seem to have walked right into the thick of a dime novel. Why on earth should anyone follow or watch me?
Holmes	We are coming to that. You have nothing else to report to us before we go into this matter?
Henry	I have lost one of my boots.
Holmes	You have lost one of your boots?
Mortimer	My dear sir, it is only mislaid. You will find it when you return to the hotel. What is the use of troubling Mr. Holmes with trifles of this kind?
Henry	Well, mislaid it, anyhow. I put them both outside my door last night, and there was only one in the morning. I could get no sense out of the fellow who cleans them. The worst of it is that I only bought the pair last night in the Strand, and I have never had them on.
Holmes	If you have never worn them, why did you put them out to be cleaned?
Henry	They were tan boots and had never been varnished. That was why I put them out.
Holmes	So on your arrival in London yesterday you went out at once and bought a pair of boots?
Henry	I did a good deal of shopping. Dr. Mortimer here went round with me. You see, if I am to be squire down there I must dress the part. Among other things I bought these brown boots and had one stolen before ever I had them on my feet.
Holmes	It seems a singularly useless thing to steal. I confess that I share Dr. Mortimer's belief that it will not be long before the missing boot is found.
Henry	And, now, gentlemen it seems to me that I have spoken quite enough about the little that I know. It is time that you kept your promise and gave me a full account of what we are all driving at.
Holmes	Your request is a very reasonable one, Dr. Mortimer, I think you should let Sir Henry read the myth to himself.
Henry	*(After reading.)* Well, I seem to have come into an inheritance with a vengeance, of course, I've heard of the hound ever since I was in the nursery.

It's the pet story of the family, though I never thought of taking it seriously before. But as to my uncle's death -- well, it all seems boiling up in my head, and I can't get it clear yet. You don't seem quite to have made up your mind whether it's a case for a policeman or a clergyman.

Holmes   Precisely.

Henry   And now there's this affair of the letter to me at the hotel. I suppose that fits into its place.

Mortimer   It seems to show that someone knows more than we do about what goes on upon the moor.

Holmes   And that someone is not ill-disposed towards you, since they warn you of danger.

Henry   Or it may be that they wish, for their own purposes, to scare me away.

Holmes   Well, of course, that is possible also. *(To Mortimer.)* I am very much indebted to you, Dr. Mortimer, for introducing me to a problem which presents several interesting alternatives. *(To Henry.)* But the practical point which we now have to decide, Sir Henry, is whether it is or is not advisable for you to go to Baskerville Hall.

Henry   Why should I not go?

Watson   There seems to be danger.

Henry   Do you mean danger from this family fiend or do you mean danger from human beings?

Holmes   Well, that is what we have to find out.

Henry   *(Determined, fiery.)* Whichever it is, my answer is fixed. There is no devil in hell, Mr. Holmes, and there is no man upon earth who can prevent me from going to the home of my own people, and you may take that to be my final answer. However, I have hardly had time to think. I should like to have a quiet hour by myself to make up my mind. I am going back right away to my hotel. I will return later. I'll be able to tell you more clearly then how this thing strikes me.

Holmes   Shall I have a cab called?

Henry   I'd prefer to walk, for this affair has flurried me rather.

Mortimer   I'll join you in a walk, with pleasure.

Holmes   Then we meet again at two o'clock. Au revoir, and good-morning! *(Mortimer and Henry leave. Holmes is suddenly, very active, looking through the window.)* Watson, *(With a little cry of satisfaction.)* come look, you will observe an Hansom Cab on the other side of the road, turning and now following slowly behind our two new friends. Do you notice anything else?

Watson   All I can see Holmes is the outline of a man with a distinctive black beard inside.

Holmes   Indeed Watson, perhaps even a false one?

Watson   Shall we follow?

Holmes   No Watson we will wait. I have taken note of the number of the cab No: 2704. We don't want to be seen as suspecting too much. A clever rouse by our opponent to place himself in a cab as it gives him cover whilst loitering and speed if Sir Henry was to take a cab himself. I have not finally made up my mind whether it is a benevolent or a malevolent agency which is in touch with us.

Watson   However, he is now at the disposal of the cabman!

Holmes   Precisely, an obvious disadvantage Watson. Could you swear to that man's face within the cab?

Watson   I could swear only to the beard.

Holmes   And so could I - from which I gather that in all probability it was a false one. A clever man upon so delicate an errand has no use for a beard save to conceal his features. *(Making a telephone call.)*... Please excuse me, Watson. I must make a call. Operator, central 241 please, District Messenger's Office. Ah, Wilson! Sherlock Holmes. Your thanks are not necessary, Wilson, the case was some months ago. However, I believe you can now repay the favour. There are 23 hotels in the immediate neighbourhood of Charing Cross. Wilson, I need both you and one of your lads to visit to each hotel. Cartwright showed remarkable ability, take him. In each case, you will inform the outside porter that an important telegram has gone missing and that you wish to search the waste paper of yesterday. Now, what you are really looking for is the leader page of yesterday's Times with some holes cut in it. The odds are enormously against your finding it, but for thirty shillings I expect you'll get through the baskets with remarkable speed. Let me have a report by wire at Baker Street before evening. *(Puts down telephone.)* And now, Watson, it only remains for us to find out by wire the identity of the cabman of No. 2704, and then we will drop into one of the Bond Street picture galleries.

Scene 3 Holmes' Office

(Henry enters office furiously with an old boot. Followed by Dr. Mortimer.)

Henry	Seems to me they are playing me for a sucker in that hotel. They'll find they've started in to monkey with the wrong man unless they are careful. If that chap can't find my missing boot there will be trouble. I can take a joke with the best, Mr. Holmes, but they've got a bit over the mark this time.
Holmes	But, surely, you said that it was a new brown boot?
Henry	So it was, sir. And now it's an old black one.
Watson	What! You don't mean to say?
Henry	That's just what I do mean to say. I only had three pairs in the world - the new brown, the old black, and the patent leathers, which I am wearing. Last night they took one of my brown ones, and to-day they have sneaked one of the black. Mr. Holmes, you'll excuse my troubling you about such a trifle -
Holmes	I don't profess to understand it yet. This case of yours is very complex, Sir Henry. We hold several threads in our hands, and the odds are that one or other of them will guide us to the truth. We may waste time in following the wrong one, but sooner or later we must come upon the right.
Henry	Well I intend to go to Baskerville Hall at the end of the week.
Holmes	I think that your decision is a wise one. I have evidence that you are being dogged in London, and in the great city it is difficult to discover who these people are or what their objective is. If their intentions are evil they might do you a mischief, and we should be powerless to prevent it. You did not know, Dr. Mortimer, that you were followed this morning from my house?
Mortimer	*(Shocked.)* Followed! By whom?
Holmes	That, unfortunately, is what I cannot tell you. Have you among your neighbours or acquaintances on Dartmoor any man with a black, full beard?
Mortimer	No - or, let me see - why, yes. Barrymore, Sir Charles's butler, is a man with a full, black beard.
Holmes	Ha! Where is Barrymore?
Mortimer	He is in charge of the Hall.
Holmes	We had best ascertain if he is really there, or if by any possibility he might be in London.
Henry	How can you do that?

Holmes	Give me a telegraph form Watson. 'Is all ready for Sir Henry?' That will do. Address to Mr. Barrymore, Baskerville Hall. What is the nearest telegraph-office?
Mortimer	Grimpen.
Holmes	We will send a second wire to the postmaster, Grimpen: 'Telegram to Mr. Barrymore to be delivered into his own hand. If absent, please return wire to Sir Henry Baskerville, Northumberland Hotel.' That should let us know before evening whether Barrymore is at his post in Devonshire or not.
Henry	By the way, Dr. Mortimer, who is this Barrymore, anyhow?
Mortimer	He is the son of the old caretaker, who is dead. They have looked after the Hall for four generations now. So far as I know, he and his wife are as respectable a couple as any in the county.
Henry	At the same time, it's clear enough that so long as there are none of the family at the Hall these people have a mighty fine home and nothing to do.
Mortimer	That is true.
Holmes	Did Barrymore profit at all by Sir Charles's will?
Mortimer	He and his wife knew they had five hundred pounds each. I hope you don't look with suspicious eyes upon everyone who received a legacy from Sir Charles, for I also had a thousand pounds left to me.
Holmes	Indeed! And anyone else?
Mortimer	There were many insignificant sums to individuals, and a large number of public charities. The residue of Seven hundred and forty thousand pounds all went to Sir Henry. The total value of the estate came close to a million.
Holmes	Dear me. I had no idea that so gigantic a sum was involved. It is a stake for which a man might well play a desperate game. And one more question, Dr. Mortimer. Supposing that anything happened to our young friend here - you will forgive the unpleasant hypothesis! Who would inherit the estate?
Mortimer	Since Rodger Baskerville, Sir Charles's youngest brother died unmarried, the estate would descend to the Desmonds, who are distant cousins. James Desmond is an elderly clergyman in Westmoreland.
Holmes	Thank you. These details are all of great interest. Have you met Mr. James Desmond?
Mortimer	Yes; he is a man of venerable appearance and of saintly life. I remember that he refused to accept any settlement from Sir Charles, though he pressed it upon him.

Watson	And this man of simple tastes would be the heir to Sir Charles's thousands.
Mortimer	He would be the heir to the estate because that is entailed. He would also be the heir to the money unless it were willed otherwise by the present owner, who can, of course, do what he likes with it.
Holmes	And have you made your will, Sir Henry?
Henry	No, Mr. Holmes, I have not. I've had no time. I feel that the money should go with the title and estate. That was my poor uncle's idea. How is the owner going to restore the glories of the Baskervilles if he has not money enough to keep up the property? House, land, and dollars must go together.
Holmes	Quite so Sir Henry now moving on, there is one provision which I must make. You certainly must not go alone. Dr. Mortimer has her practice to attend to, and her house is miles away from yours. Sir Henry, you must take a trusty man, who will be always by your side. At present one of the most revered names in England is being besmirched by a blackmailer, and only I can stop a disastrous scandal. You will see how impossible it is for me to go to Dartmoor.
Henry	Whom would you recommend, then?
Holmes	*(Laying his hand on Watson's shoulder.)* There is no man who is better worth having at your side than Watson when you are in a tight place. No one can say so more confidently than I.
Henry	*(Shaking Watson's hand.)* Well, now, that is real kind of you, Dr. Watson, will you come?
Watson	I will come, with pleasure, I do not know how I could employ my time better.
Henry	Then on Saturday morning unless you hear to the contrary we three shall meet at Paddington Station, at 9. Good day to you. *(Mortimer and Sir Henry exit).*
Watson	Goodbye.
Holmes	*(To Watson.)* And you will report very carefully to me. When a crisis comes, as it will do, I will direct how you shall act. You must keep me up to date by telegram or letter. Does that suit Dr. Watson?
Watson	Perfectly. *(To the audience)* The telegrams were sent and then, an hour later there was a knock at the door.
	(Knock at the door. Maid enters with three telegrams.)
Watson	Three Telegrams.
Holmes	Read them to me Watson, if you'd be so kind.

Watson	The first runs: One boot miraculously found under bed. Stop. No sign of other, very peculiar. Stop. Just heard Barrymore is at Hall. Stop. *HENRY.*
Holmes	Interesting.
Watson	The second: Visited twenty-three hotels as directed, sorry to report unable to trace cut sheet of Times. Stop. *WILSON AND CARTWRIGHT.*
Holmes	There go my threads, Watson. There is nothing more stimulating than a case where everything goes against you. We must cast round for another scent.
Watson	Ah huh! The third telegram is from the cabman who drove the spy. It reads: Message from head office Mr Sherlock Holmes inquiring about cab 2704 stop Am confused as fair paid to use cab most of day informed me he was detective by name of Sherlock Holmes stop. Put him at forty, average height, dressed smart, thick black beard stop. Eye colour unknown stop. *JOHN CLAYTON*, The Borough.
Holmes	*(Silent amazement then in a burst of laughter.)* A touch, Watson -- an undeniable touch! I feel a foil as quick and supple as my own. So his name was Sherlock Holmes, was it? The cunning rascal! I tell you, Watson, this time we have got a foeman who is worthy of our steel. I've been checkmated in London. I can only wish you better luck in Devonshire. But I'm not easy in my mind about it.
Watson	About what?
Holmes	About sending you. It's an ugly business, Watson, an ugly dangerous business, and the more I see of it the less I like it. Yes my dear fellow, you may laugh, but I give you my word that I shall be very glad to have you back safe and sound in Baker Street once more. I wish you to report facts in the fullest possible manner to me, and you can leave me to do the theorizing.
Watson	What sort of facts?
Holmes	Anything which may seem to have a bearing however indirect upon the case, and especially the relations between young Baskerville and his neighbours or any fresh particulars concerning the death of Sir Charles. One thing only appears to be certain, and that is that Mr. James Desmond, who is the next heir, is an elderly gentleman of a very amiable disposition. I really think that we may eliminate him entirely from our calculations. I want facts about the people who will actually be surrounding Sir Henry Baskerville upon the moor.
Watson	Would it not be well in the first place to get rid of this Barrymore couple?
Holmes	By no means. You could not make a greater mistake. If they are innocent it would be a cruel injustice, and if they are guilty we should be giving up all chance of bringing it home to them. No, no, we will preserve them upon our list of suspects. Then there is a groom at the Hall, if I remember right. There is our friend Dr. Mortimer, whom I believe to be entirely honest. There is this

naturalist, Stapleton, and there is his sister, who is said to be a young lady of attractions. There is Mr. Frankland, of Lafter Hall, who is also an unknown factor. These are the folk who must be your very special study.

Watson   I will do my best.

Holmes   Tell Sir Henry to bear in mind, the phrase in that queer old legend to avoid the moor in those hours of darkness when the powers of evil are exalted. And keep your revolver near you night and day, and never relax your precautions. And now to visit one of the Bond Street picture galleries.

Scene 4 Village Green, The Outskirts of Dartmoor

(Train whistle, steam, door opening and shutting. Sir Henry, Watson and Mortimer enter and get caught up in a country Harvest Festival Fair and the following performance. MUSIC. YOKELS AND COMEDIANS ENTER. ALL ACTORS APART FROM MORTIMER, WATSON, HOLMES AND SIR HENRY.....(ie. Selden, Maria, Mr and Mrs Barrymore, Laura or other extras. They perform the 'legend' in a basic yokel style, silly and funny. Twiddling moustaches etc.)

Yokel   *Hear Ye! Hear Ye... In honour of Sir Charles Baskerville. God Rest His Soul.*

The Myth of the Baskervilles melodramatic, funny and Improvised

Yokels   This horrible history did start one day

When birds and deer were out to play

The flowers bloomed and the brook did bubble.

Nobody knew there was going to be trouble,

When a handsome squire did court a girl.

And wanted very much to take her pearl.

She flirted innocently at first

Then suddenly she saw him at his worst!

Hugo the tyrant he became.

All she could feel was terrible shame.

Hugo the tyrant he always was,

Treating young girls as though they were whores!

Now honest audience you know what we mean,

That sometimes men can get very keen.

So in an impulse he swept her away

And locked her up for a night and a day.

His garret was dark and dingy and cold

But she wasn't only pretty she was so bold.

She could hear him and his friends carousing

And she could sense that he was arousing.

So she took her chance and slid down the ivy

Which at that time was not very tidy!

It caught her dress and tore her skirt,

But she wasn't going to let it hurt.

Watson   I do believe this rings a very recent bell Sir Henry. Pray do you recognise the story they are acting out?

Sir Henry   Good Heavens it's the old Baskerville Curse!

Yokels   Hugo was primed and ready to go

Fuelled by the booze his lust did grow.

But opening the door to her soggy cell

He found that things were not very well.

He charged up his 13 friends to ride

They all raced out to bring back her hide.

The moor was ghostly cold and misty

He still was feeling awfully frisky.

That Baskerville the wicked rascal

Chased the beauty out of his castle.

He set his doggy hounds upon her

So he could try to take her honour.

One hound led the pack all sinew and fur.

Sir Hugo directed it to run down her.

They chased her all over that scary moor.

She leaped into crag and onto a tor.

He rendered his body and soul to what's evil

And all of his powers were every inch devil.

Then in the distance came a braying howl

A sound most terrible and most foul.

'Is that a hound?' His mates whispered under their breath.

Praying so hard and avoiding their death.

Hugo the brute with no care stormed ahead.

Soon though, however, they all found him dead.

Discovered his corpse lying close to the lady

Something was looking ever so shady.

Hugo the tyrant was not anymore

Hugo the tyrant had died on that more.

His throat was cut open wide with a gash

The beast shook his body as though it was trash

Fire flashed from its teeth its body did glow.

Eyes shining, his phosphorus s'liva did flow.

From that day forth the legend grew,

That all the heirs to the squire Hugoo

Would die by the teeth of that spectral hound

And paw marks of green would always be found.

Their bodies, discovered dead and contorted.

As though an electric current had shorted.

Nobody wanted to visit the moor

There was no tranquil peace any more.

And to this day we won't go alone

Because of the story we have shown.

We pay our respects to Sir Charles our good Lord

And act out this show with great accord.

We're waiting to see our new young baronette.

Cos we haven't had a chance to meet him yet.

Mrs B   Wait a minute ladies look at the time

I am going to have to leave this rhyme.

I think Sir Henry is there in the crowd

I've got to get home to make him proud.

Baskerville Hall is beckoning me back,

As our new Lord will need to unpack.

Bye for now I've had so much fun

I am really going to have to run, run, run.

All	We wish Sire great happiness, luck and health.
	He will definitely have to have some stealth
	To avoid the Baskerville deadly curse.
	A Shake and a shiver - what could be worse?
	Now Good day to you audience one and all
	Thank you for this we have had a ball.

(After the show depicting the myth Mortimer, Watson and Henry start to walk around the auditorium.)

Mortimer	Although somewhat innocent that was amusing and proves, like I said, how the locals feel that it is part of their heritage.
Watson	Have you visited the hall before Sir Henry?
Henry	I was a boy in my teens at the time of my father's death so I've never seen it. For he lived in a little cottage on the South Coast. Thence I went straight to a friend in America. I tell you it is all as new to me as it is to you, Dr. Watson, and I'm as keen as possible to see the moor. (Lights fading)
Mortimer	There is your first view of the moor. *(Bell ringing.)*
Sir Henry	What is that noise
Yokel	It's the bell warning us of the escaped prisoner on the moor. He disappeared a few days ago and is believed to be hiding out somewhere up there. The soldiers and warders are looking for him.
Watson	Who is the prisoner?
Yokel	The notorious Selden. He's said to cut the throats of his victims. They ring the bell to remind us to lock up our houses well at dusk. I'll be off Sire.
Mortimer	We must hurry it is getting dark.
Watson	I remember the case well, for Holmes took an interest on account of the peculiar ferocity of the crime. The commutation of his death sentence had been due to some doubts as to his complete sanity.
Mortimer	Thank goodness we've arrived at Baskerville Hall!
Henry	It's magnificent though it glimmers like a ghost. Was it here that it happened?

Mortimer	No, no, the yew alley is on the other side.
Henry	It's no wonder my uncle felt as if trouble were coming on him in such a place as this, it's enough to scare any man. I'll have a row of electric lamps up here inside of six months, and you won't know it again, with a thousand candlepower Swan and Edison right here in front of the hall door. It's still draped in ivy as in the legend.
Mortimer	See how from this central block the twin towers rise, ancient and crenelated, like a castle. There are modern wings of black granite to the left and right of the towers.
Henry	Who's in the Hall? There's a light flickering in the mullioned windows.
Mortimer	I asked the Barrymores to light a fire and put on the lights.
Barrymore	*(At the edge of the stage.)* Welcome, Sir Henry! Welcome to Baskerville Hall! *(Mrs B. joins him to help with the bags).*
Mortimer	You don't mind if I go straight home, Sir Henry? It's getting dark.
Henry	Surely you will stay and have some dinner?
Mortimer	No, I must go. I shall probably find some work awaiting me. I would stay to show you over the house, but Barrymore will be a better guide than I. Good-bye, and never hesitate night or day to send for me if I can be of service.

Scene 5 Inside Baskerville Hall

(Lighting should create long shadows.)

Henry   Let's warm ourselves by the fire. It's just as I imagined it. Is it not the very picture of an old ancestral home? To think that this should be the same hall in which for five hundred years my people have lived. It strikes me solemn to think of it.

(Barrymore stands in front of us now with the subdued manner of a well-trained servant. He's a remarkable-looking man, tall, handsome, with a black beard and pale, distinguished features.)

Barrymore   Would you wish dinner to be served at once, sir?

Henry   Is it ready?

Barrymore   In a very few minutes, sir. You will find hot water in your rooms. My wife and I will be happy, Sir Henry, to stay with you until you have made your fresh arrangements, but you will understand that under the new conditions this house will require a considerable staff.

Henry   What new conditions?

Barrymore   I only meant, sir, that Sir Charles led a very retired life, and we were able to look after his wants. You would, naturally, wish to have more company, and so you will need changes in your household.

Henry   Do you mean that your wife and you wish to leave?

Barrymore   Only when it is quite convenient to you, sir.

Henry   But your family have been with us for several generations, have they not? I should be sorry to begin my life here by breaking an old family connection.

Barrymore   *(Concerned.)* I feel that also, sir, and so does my wife. But to tell the truth, sir, we were both very much attached to Sir Charles and his death gave us a shock and made these surroundings very painful to us. I fear that we shall never again be easy in our minds at Baskerville Hall.

Henry   But what do you intend to do?

Barrymore   I have no doubt, sir, that we shall succeed in establishing ourselves in some business. Sir Charles's generosity has given us the means to do so. And now, sir, perhaps I had best show you to your rooms.

Henry   *(W. and H. get up and look around. Henry shivering.)*I don't wonder that my uncle got a little jumpy if he lived all alone in such a house as this. However, if it suits you, Watson, we will retire early to-night, and perhaps things may seem more cheerful in the morning.

(They all exit... Lights down, stage almost dark, sound of clocks chiming, long pause the sob of a woman.)

Scene 6 Inside Baskerville Hall

(Baskerville Hall daylight, birds singing everything bright. Mrs Barrymore brings in a pot of tea. Barrymore stands nearby.)

Henry   I guess it is ourselves and not the house that we have to blame! We were tired with our journey and chilled by our drive, so we took a grey view of the place. Now we are fresh and well, so it is all cheerful once more.

Watson   And yet it was not entirely a question of imagination. Did you, for example, happen to hear someone, a woman I think, sobbing in the night?

Henry   That is curious, for I did when I was half asleep fancy that I heard something of the sort. I waited quite a time, but there was no more of it, so I concluded that it was all a dream.

Watson   I heard it distinctly, and I am sure that it was the sob of a woman.

Barrymore There are only two women in the house, Sir Henry. One is the scullery-maid, who sleeps in the other wing. The other is my wife, and I can answer for it that the sound could not have come from her. *(Exits.)*

Watson   *(Pause.)* It is my belief Sir Henry that Barrymore has just lied. I observed Mrs Barrymore to have red swollen eyes. Her husband must know. It was Barrymore who found the body and he does have a beard just like the man in the cab who followed you in London. A visit to the Grimpen post office is called for to see if the test telegram we sent really was placed in Barrymore's hand. I shall then report back to Holmes.

Scene 7 Post Office

(Scene change. The postmaster/mistress is also the village grocer, vegetables on counter. Lights up Stage Right.)

Postmistress	Certainly, sir, I had the telegram delivered to Mr. Barrymore exactly as directed.
Watson	Who delivered it?
Postmistress	Our boy, James, delivered that telegram to Mr. Barrymore at the Hall last week.
Watson	Into his own hands?
Postmistress	He said he was up in the loft at the time, but he gave it to Mrs. Barrymore who promised to deliver it at once.
Watson	Did he actually see Mr. Barrymore?
Postmistress	No, sir; I tell you he was in the loft.
Watson	If he didn't see him, how did he know he was in the loft?
Postmistress	Well, surely his own wife ought to know where he is! Didn't he get the telegram? If there is any mistake it is for Mr. Barrymore himself to complain. Good day to you Sir. *(Freeze or exit.)*
Watson	Good day. *(Under his breath to audience.)* So if Barrymore wasn't there he could indeed have been in London. But why? The only thing I could fathom is that if the Baskervilles vacated the Hall then the Barrymores could lead a very comfortable life living there by themselves. I needed to talk to Holmes. *(Starts to walk away.)*

Scene 8 The Moor

(On the Moor across front of stage no scene change. Enter Stapleton, butterfly-net in one of his hand, perhaps a tin of specimens.)

Stapleton	You will, I am sure, excuse my presumption, Dr. Watson. Here on the moor we are homely folk and do not wait for formal introductions. I am Jack Stapleton, of Merripit House.
Watson	How did you know me?
Stapleton	I have been calling on Dr.Mortimer, and she pointed you out to me from the window of her surgery as you passed. I trust that Sir Henry is none the worse for his journey?
Watson	He is very well, thank you.

(Walking back to Hall across down stage. Arrive during conversation.)

Stapleton	I need not tell you that it means a very great deal to the locals that Sir Henry has come to live here. He has no superstitious fears in the matter?
Watson	I do not think that it is likely. Do come in. *(enter SL as if back door of Hall)*
Stapleton	Of course you know the legend of the fiend dog which haunts the family?
Watson	I have heard it.
Stapleton	The story took a great hold upon the imagination of Sir Charles, and I have no doubt that it led to his tragic end.
Watson	But how?
Stapleton	His nerves were so worked up that the appearance of any dog might have had a fatal effect upon his diseased heart. I fancy that he really did see something of the kind upon that last night in the yew alley. I feared that some disaster might occur, for I was very fond of the old man, and I knew that his heart was weak.
Watson	How did you know that?
Stapleton	He told me himself.
Watson	You think, then, that some dog pursued Sir Charles, and that he died of fright in consequence?
Stapleton	Have you any better explanation?
Watson	I have not come to any conclusion.

Stapleton   Has Mr. Sherlock Holmes? *(Watson looks shocked.)* We all know you Dr Watson for being Holmes right hand man. When, Dr. Mortimer told me your name she could not deny your identity. If you are here, then it follows that Mr. Sherlock Holmes is interesting himself in the matter, and I am naturally curious to know what view he may take. *(continue straight into next scene.)*

Scene 9 Baskerville Hall *(They are already there.)*

Watson   I am afraid that I cannot answer that question.

Stapleton   May I ask if he is going to honour us with a visit himself?

Watson   He cannot leave town at present. He has other cases which engage his attention.

Stapleton   What a pity! He might throw some light on that which is so dark to us. But as to your own researches, if there is any possible way in which I can be of service to you I trust that you will command me.

Watson   I assure you that I am simply here upon a visit to my friend, Sir Henry, and that I need no help of any kind.

Stapleton   You are perfectly right to be wary and discreet. I promise you that I will not mention the matter again. It is a wonderful place, the moor, I never tire of the moor. You cannot think the wonderful secrets which it contains. It is so vast, and so barren, and so mysterious.

Watson   You know it well then?

Stapleton   I have only been here two years. The residents would call me a newcomer. We came shortly after Sir Charles settled. I've explored every part of the country and I should think that there are few men who know it better than I do.

Watson   Is it hard to know?

Stapleton   Very hard. You see, for example, that great plain to the north here with the queer hills breaking out of it. *(Looking out of window towards audience or upstage.)* Do you observe anything remarkable about that?

Watson   It would be a rare place for a gallop.

Stapleton   The very thought has cost several people their lives. You notice those bright green spots scattered thickly over it?

Watson   Yes, they seem more fertile than the rest.

Stapleton   *(Laughing.)* That is the great Grimpen Mire. A false step means death to man or beast. Only yesterday I saw one of the moor ponies wander into it. He never came out. I saw his head for quite a long time, but it sucked him down at last. Even in dry seasons it is a danger to cross it, but after these autumn rains it is an awful place. And yet I can find my way to the very heart of it and return alive. Yes, it's a bad place, the Grimpen Mire.

Watson   And you say you can penetrate it?

Stapleton	There are one or two paths which a very active man can take. I have found them out.
Watson	But why should you wish to go into so horrible a place?
Stapleton	Well, you see the hills beyond? They are really islands cut off on all sides by the impassable mire, which has crawled round them in the course of years. That is where the rare plants and the butterflies are, if you have the wit to reach them.
Watson	I shall try my luck some day.
Stapleton	For God's sake put such an idea out of your mind. I assure you that there would not be the least chance of your coming back alive. It is only by remembering certain complex landmarks that I am able to do it.

(Hound//Bitton howls.)

Watson	What is that?
Stapleton	Queer place, the moor!
Watson	Yes, but what is it?
Stapleton	The peasants say it is the Hound of the Baskervilles calling for its prey. I've heard it once or twice before, but never quite so loud.
Watson	You are an educated man. You don't believe such nonsense as that? What do you think is the cause of so strange a sound?
Stapleton	Bogs make queer noises sometimes. It's the mud settling, or the water rising, or something.
Watson	No, no, that was a living voice.
Stapleton	Well, perhaps it was. Did you ever hear a bittern booming?
Watson	No, I never did.
Stapleton	It's a very rare bird, practically extinct, in England now. Yes, I should not be surprised to learn that what we have heard is the cry of the last of the Bitterns. What do you make of those over there? *(Pointing to stones out of the window.)*
Watson	The slope's covered with grey circular rings of stone, there's at least 20 of them. What are they? Sheep-pens?
Stapleton	No, they are the homes of our worthy ancestors. Prehistoric man lived on the moor, and as no one in particular has lived there since, we find all his little arrangements exactly as he left them.

Watson	But it is quite a town. When was it inhabited?
Stapleton	Neolithic man - no date. He grazed his cattle on these slopes, and he learned to dig for tin when the bronze sword began to supersede the stone axe. Look at the great trench in the opposite hill. That is his mark. Yes, you will find some very singular points about the moor, Dr. Watson. Oh, excuse me an instant! It is surely Cyclopides. *(Seeing a butterfly out of the window he lifts his butterfly net, goes off stage SL.)*
Maria	Go back! *(Running on USR.)* Go straight back to London, instantly.
Mrs B	*(Hurriedly following behind Maria)* I'm sorry Sir, she rushed straight past, I couldn't stop her –
Watson	Please don't worry Mrs Barrymore, thank you.
	(Mrs Barrymore exits)
Watson	Madam! Why should I go back?
Maria	I cannot explain. But for God's sake do what I ask you. Go back and never set foot upon the moor again.
Watson	But I have only just come. Miss Stapleton I assume?
Maria	Can you not tell when a warning is for your own good? Go back to London! Start to-night! Get away from this place at all costs! Hush, my brother is coming! Not a word of what I have said. He hum, it's rather late in the year to see the beauties of the place.
Stapleton	*(Re-entering SL)* Oh! Hello Maria.
Maria	Well, Jack, you are very hot.
Stapleton	Yes, I was chasing a Cyclopides. He is very rare and seldom found in the late autumn. What a pity that I should have missed him! *(Eyes glancing from Maria to Watson.)* You have introduced yourselves, I can see.
Maria	Yes. I was telling Sir Henry that it was rather late for him to see the true beauties of the moor.
Watson	No, my name is Dr. Watson. My dear, I am Sir Henry's friend.
Maria	*(Vexed.)* We have been talking at cross purposes. I talked as if Dr. Watson were a resident instead of being merely a visitor. But you will come, will you not, and see Merripit House?
Stapleton	You'll think it's a strange spot to have chosen, but we manage to make ourselves fairly happy, do we not, Maria?

Maria	Quite happy. *(Unconvinced.)*
Stapleton	I had a school, in the North Country. The work to a man of my temperament was mechanical and uninteresting, but the privilege of living with youth, of helping to mould those young minds, was a gift. However, the fates were against us. A serious epidemic broke out in the school and three of the boys died. It never recovered from the blow, and much of my capital was irretrievably swallowed up. So we moved to satisfy my strong tastes for botany and zoology, I find an unlimited field of work here, and my sister is as devoted to Nature as I am.
Watson	It certainly did cross my mind that it might be a little dull - less for you, perhaps, than for your sister.
Maria	*(Too quickly.)* No, no, I am never dull.
Stapleton	We have books, we have our studies, and we have interesting neighbours. Dr. Mortimer is most learned. Poor Sir Charles was also an admirable companion. We knew him well and miss him more than I can tell. I'm sorry Sir Henry isn't here to be introduced to. Are you coming Maria?
Maria	I'll catch up with you in a minute. *(He goes.)* I came here to make the acquaintance of Sir Henry. I must be quick. I wanted to say to you how sorry I am about the stupid mistake I made in thinking that you were Sir Henry. Please forget the words I said, which have no application whatever to you.
Watson	But I can't forget them, Miss Stapleton, I am Sir Henry's friend, and his welfare is a very close concern of mine. Tell me why it was that you were so eager that Sir Henry should return to London?
Maria	A woman's whim, Dr. Watson. When you know me better you will understand that I cannot always give reasons for what I say or do.
Watson	No, no. I remember the intensity in your voice, the look in your eyes. Please, please, be frank with me, Miss Stapleton. Tell me what it was that you meant, and I will promise to convey your warning to Sir Henry.
Maria	You make too much of it, Dr. Watson. My brother and I were very much shocked by the death of Sir Charles. We knew him very well, for his favourite walk was over the moor to our house. He was deeply impressed with the curse which hung over the family, and when this tragedy came I naturally felt that there must be some grounds for the fears which he had expressed. I was distressed therefore when another member of the family came down to live here, and I felt that he should be warned of the danger which he will run.
Watson	But what is the danger?
Maria	You know the story of the hound?
Watson	I do not believe in such nonsense.

Maria	But I do. If you have any influence with Sir Henry, take him away from a place which has always been fatal to his family.
Watson	I fear that unless you can give me some more definite information than this it would be impossible to get him to move.
Maria	I cannot say anything definite, for I do not know anything definite.
Watson	I would ask you one more question, Miss Stapleton. If you meant no more than this when you first spoke to me, why should you not wish your brother to overhear what you said?
Maria	My brother is very anxious to have the Hall inhabited, for he thinks it is for the good of the poor folk upon the moor. He would be very angry if he knew that I have said anything which might induce Sir Henry to go away. I have done my duty now, I must go. Goodbye.

Scene 10 Baskerville Hall

(Lights on Watson at desk SL or he can stand.)

Watson   Baskerville Hall, October 13th.... My dear Holmes:

I trust you have received my previous letters and telegrams about this most God-forsaken corner of the world. The longer one stays here the more does the spirit of the moor sinks into one's soul, its vastness, and also its grim charm. This is of no interest to your discerning mind, however, so here are the facts.

A fortnight has passed since the escaped convict's flight, during which time he has not been seen and nothing has been heard of him. There are plenty of places to hide but there is nothing to eat, unless he were to catch and slaughter one of the moor sheep. He may have gone but we cannot be sure. I worry for the Stapletons. Jack Stapleton is not a very strong man and they live miles from anyone. They would be helpless in the hands of this desperate criminal. They dine here tonight and there is some talk of our going to them next week.

Our friend, the baronet, begins to display a considerable interest in our fair neighbour. There is something tropical and exotic about Maria which forms a singular contrast to her brother. He has certainly a marked influence over her, for I have seen her continually glance at him as she talks, as if seeking approbation for what she's said. I trust that he is kind to her, yet I am certain that he does not wish her intimacy with Sir Henry to ripen into love.

A few days ago, Jack took us to a short valley between rugged tors where the legend of the wicked Hugo is said to have its origin. In the middle of an open, grassy space rose two great stones, worn and sharpened until they looked like the huge corroding fangs of some monstrous beast. He told Sir Henry and I of similar cases, where several families had suffered from some evil influence and he left us with the impression that he shared the popular view upon the matter.

On Thursday, Dr Mortimer showed us the yew alley. It is a long, dismal walk, and I imagined, as the old man stood by the gate, he saw something which terrified him so that he lost his wits and ran and ran until he died of sheer horror and exhaustion. Was it a spectral hound, silent, and monstrous? Did Barrymore know more than he cared to say? I am certain there is the dark shadow of crime behind it.

One other neighbour whom I have met since I wrote last is Mr. Frankland of Lafter Hall, who lives some miles to the south of us. He is an elderly man with a passion for the British law. He sees all that happens as he has an excellent telescope with which he lies upon the roof of his own house and sweeps the moor all day in the hope of catching a glimpse of the escaped convict.

Let me end with the Barrymores and the surprising development of last night. Firstly, about the test telegram. I told Sir Henry what I'd learned from the postmistress and he at once had Barrymore up....*(moves SL)*

Scene 11 Baskerville Hall

(Lights up in Hall.)

Henry   Was the telegram delivered into your own hands?

Barrymore   No, *(Surprised.)* I was in the box-room at the time, and my wife brought it up to me.

Henry   Did you answer it yourself?

Barrymore   No; I told my wife what to answer and she went down to write it.*(Pause)....*I do not quite understand the object of your questions, Sir Henry, I trust that they do not mean that I have done anything to forfeit your confidence?

Henry   My dear Barrymore I apologise I assure you, you have done nothing wrong. Indeed to prove I hold nothing against you I intend to give you a considerable part of my old wardrobe, now that the London outfits have all arrived!

Barrymore   Sir Henry, that is most kind but I'm not sure I can accept such a generous offer.

Henry   I absolutely insist. Go to my chamber and take them. *(Barrymore exits.)*

Watson   *(Writing again.)* Mrs. Barrymore is of interest to me. She is intensely respectable though inclined to be puritanical. However, I have more than once observed traces of tears upon her face. Sometimes I suspect Barrymore of being a domestic tyrant. I have always felt that there was something singular and questionable in this man's character, but the adventure of last night brought all my suspicions to a head.....

             (Lights change...... a corridor of light from the side or high up like the moon, from the window if there is one. Owls hooting. The howl of a dog. Barrymore prowls through the hall furtively. Being very careful not to be heard. Watson watches him. B. looks out of the window and appears to sign with his torch/lantern, creepy.)

Barrymore   Groans heavily (*Exits. Perhpas the sound of a door opening/creaking or a lock turning in the distance.)*

ACT 2   Scene 1 Baskerville Hall

Baskerville Hall, Oct. 15th.

Watson   MY DEAR HOLMES:

Things have taken a turn which I could not have anticipated. In some ways they have within the last forty-eight hours become much clearer and in some ways they have become more complicated. But I will tell you all and you shall judge for yourself.

The window Barrymore was looking through last night has the best view of the moor between an avenue of trees. It struck me that it was possible that some love intrigue was afoot. The man is a striking-looking fellow, very well equipped to steal the heart of a country girl, and this would explain his wife's behaviour. Did he go out on the moor? Was the sound of the door him going out to rendezvous with someone?

I could not bear the responsibility of keeping these suspicions to myself so I had an interview with the baronet after breakfast, and I told him all that I had seen.

Act 2 Scene 2 Baskerville Hall (Daytime)

Henry   I knew that Barrymore walked about nights, and I had a mind to speak to him about it. Two or three times I have heard his steps in the passage, coming and going, just about the hour you name.

Watson   Perhaps then he pays a visit every night to that particular window.

Henry   Perhaps he does. If so, we should be able to shadow him and see what it is that he is after. I wonder what your friend Holmes would do if he were here.

Watson   I believe that he would do exactly what you now suggest. He would follow Barrymore and see what he did.

Henry   Then we shall do it together. We'll sit up in my room to-night and wait until he passes. (*Animated and excited, then puts on his hat to go out. Watson goes for his hat*.) What, are you coming, Watson? (Annoyed.)

Watson   That depends on whether you are going out on the moor.

Henry   Yes, I am.

Watson   Well, you know what my instructions are. I am sorry to intrude, but you heard how earnestly Holmes insisted that I should not leave you, and especially that you should not go alone upon the moor.

Henry   My dear fellow, Holmes, with all his wisdom, did not foresee some things which have happened since I have been on the moor. You understand me? I am sure that you are the last man in the world who would wish to be a spoil-sport. I must go out alone. (*Exits with cane.*)

Act 2 Scene 3 The Moor

Watson   *(The stage is being emptied as he speaks, changing into the moor...W.'s desk still stage left where he sits.)*

I had to follow discreetly. I caught up with him on the moor path about a quarter of a mile off. He was with Miss Stapleton. All I could do was watch from that distance. I saw them walking slowly along in deep conversation with a warmth between them, and Maria making quick little movements of her hands, anxious. Sir Henry put his arm round Maria but she pulled away from him with her face averted. He went to kiss her but they sprung apart as Stapleton appeared from nowhere and ran wildly towards them with his face grave and angry. Eventually Stapleton turned upon his heel, beckoned to his sister and, giving up, she followed and walked off with her brother. Henry stood for a minute looking after them then walked slowly back the way that he had come, his head hanging dejectedly.

(Watson gets up from desk and joins the actual scene. Desk is taken off.)

Henry   Halloa! Watson? Where have you dropped from? You don't mean to say that you came after me in spite of all?

Watson   How could I remain behind? I had no choice I had to follow you, you are my responsibility. I'm afraid I witnessed everything.

Henry   *(Disarmed by W's frankness)* You would have thought the middle of a prairie a fairly safe place for a man to be private, but, by thunder, the whole countryside seems to have been out to see me do my wooing -- and a mighty poor wooing at that! Where had you engaged a seat?

Watson   I was on that tor.

Henry   Quite in the back row, eh? But her brother was well up to the front. Did you see him come out on us?

Watson   Yes, I did.

Henry   Did he ever strike you as being crazy - this brother of hers?

Watson   I can't say that he ever did.

Henry   I dare say not. I always thought him sane enough until to-day. What's the matter with him, what's the matter with me? You've lived near me for some weeks, Watson. Tell me straight, now! Is there anything that would prevent me from making a good husband to a woman that I loved?

Watson   I should say not.

Henry	He can't object to my worldly position, so it must be myself that he has this down on. What has he against me? I never hurt man or woman in my life that I know of. And yet he would not so much as let me touch the tips of her fingers.
Watson	Did he say so?
Henry	That, and a deal more. I tell you, Watson! From the first moment I felt that she was made for me, and I swear she too is happy when she is with me. There's a light in a woman's eyes that speaks louder than words. It was only to-day for the first time that I saw a chance of having a few words with her alone. She was glad to meet me, but she would not talk about love. She kept coming back to saying this was a place of danger, and that she would never be happy until I'd left it. I told her the only way to work it was for her to arrange to go with me. With that I offered in as many words to marry her, but before she could answer, Jack came running down like a madman. What was I doing with the lady? How dared I offer her attentions which were distasteful to her? Did I think that because I was a baronet I could do what I liked? If he had not been her brother I should have known better how to answer him. As it was I told him that I hoped that she might honour me by becoming my wife. That seemed to make the matter no better, so then I lost my temper too, and I answered him rather more hotly than I should, perhaps. So it ended up with his going off with her, leaving me puzzled and bewildered. Just tell me what it all means, Watson?
Watson	I don't understand at all. Your fortune, character, age and appearance are all in your favour. He seems not to take his sister's feelings into account and has no control over his temper.

(Enter Stapleton running.)

Stapleton	Sir Henry, Dr Watson, I wish to apologise for my dissatisfactory behaviour. My only defence, Sir Henry, is that I had no idea you were becoming close with my sister. Seeing you together on the moor so intimately shocked me. I have always lead a very lonely life with Maria being my only companion, the sudden thought of losing her led to my unforgivable behaviour. May I suggest, so I have time to adjust and you have time to get to know her, if I withdraw all opposition on my part would you promise to let the matter rest for three months and to be content with cultivating the lady's friendship during that time without claiming her love?
Henry	Well it's difficult to forget the look in your eyes when you ran at me, but I must allow that no man could make a more handsome apology than you have done. So I promise to do as you ask.
Stapleton	Do please come and dine at Merripit House next Friday as a sign of it.
Henry	I will indeed and look forward to it. See you then. *(Shake hands.)* Come Watson let's walk back to Baskerville Hall. *(Stapleton exits. Henry and Watson walk, sound of owls. Lights fading.)*

Act 2 Scene 4 The Moor (Evening)

Watson	It's getting dark already. Is it just that the heavy clouds are covering any light from the moon or the stars, or is this not normal?
Henry	It's a fog coming down very quickly, we must get back as soon as possible.
Watson	What's that light? Is it a candle in the window? Or a lantern, perhaps?
Henry	Confound the man! It's Barrymore. We'll catch him red handed! No need to wait up in my room tonight now. Look....he's come down and he's coming out of the back door of the hall into the gardens.
Watson	Was he signalling to someone on the moor?
Henry	What are you doing here, Barrymore?
Barrymore	Nothing, sir. *(Can hardly speak.)* I go round at night to see that the doors and windows are fastened.
Henry	One minute we saw you on the second floor and now you're outside! Look here, Barrymore, we have made up our minds to have the truth out of you, so it will save you trouble to tell it sooner rather than later. Come, now! No lies! What were you doing at that window?
Barrymore	I was doing no harm, sir. I was holding a candle to the window.
Henry	And why were you holding a candle to the window?
Barrymore	Don't ask me, Sir Henry - don't ask me! *(Trembling.)* I give you my word, sir, that it is not my secret, and that I cannot tell it. If it concerned no one but myself I would not try to keep it from you.
Watson	He was holding it as a signal. Let us see. Let's see if there is any answer...ah ha there it is!
Barrymore	No, no, sir, it is nothing - nothing at all! I assure you, sir –
Henry	Move your light across Watson! See, the other moves also! Now, you rascal, do you deny that it is a signal? Come, speak up! Who is your confederate out yonder, and what is this conspiracy that is going on?
Barrymore	It is my business, and not yours. I will not tell. *(Enter Mrs. Barrymore.)*
Henry	Then you leave my employment right away.
Barrymore	Very good, sir. If I must I must.

Henry	And you go in disgrace. By God, you may well be ashamed of yourself. Your family has lived with mine for over a hundred years, and here I find you deep in some dark plot against me.
Mrs B.	No, no, sir; no, not against you!
Barrymore	We have to go, Eliza. This is the end of it. You can pack our things.
Mrs B	Oh, John, John, have I brought you to this? It is my doing, Sir Henry - all mine. He has done nothing except for my sake and because I asked him.
Henry	Speak out, then! What does it mean?
Mrs B	My unhappy brother is starving on the moor. We cannot let him perish at our very gates. The light is a signal to him that food is ready for him, and his light out yonder is to show the spot to which to bring it.
Watson	Then your brother is –
Mrs B	The escaped convict, sir, Selden, the criminal.
Barrymore	That's the truth, sir, I said that it was not my secret and that I could not tell it to you. But now you have heard it, and you will see that if there was a plot it was not against you.
Watson	I am amazed. Is it possible that such a respectable person is of the same blood as one of the most notorious criminals in the country?
Mrs B	Yes, sir, my name was Selden, and he is my younger brother. We humoured him too much when he was a lad and gave him his own way in everything until he came to think that the world was made for his pleasure, and that he could do what he liked in it. Then as he grew older he met wicked companions, and the devil entered into him until he broke my mother's heart and dragged our name in the dirt. From crime to crime he sank lower and lower until it is only the mercy of God which has snatched him from the scaffold; but to me, sir, he was always the little curly-headed boy that I had nursed and played with as an elder sister would. That was why he broke prison, sir. He knew that I was here and that we could not refuse to help him. When he dragged himself here one night, weary and starving, with the warders hard at his heels, what could we do? We took him in and fed him and cared for him. Then you arrived, sir, and my brother thought he would be safer on the moor than anywhere else until the hue and cry was over, so he lay in hiding there. Every day we hoped that he was gone, but as long as he was there we could not desert him. That is the whole truth, as I am an honest Christian woman and you will see that if there is blame in the matter it does not lie with my husband but with me, for whose sake he has done what he has.
Henry	Is this true, Barrymore?
Barrymore	Yes, Sir Henry. Every word of it.

Henry	Well, I cannot blame you for standing by your own wife. Forget what I have said. Go to your room, you two, and we shall talk further about this matter in the morning.

(The Barrymores exit)

Henry	Selden cannot be far if Barrymore had to carry out the food to him. And this villain is waiting beside that light which is less than a mile away. Watson, I am going out there to take that man!
Watson	Quite right old man absolutely we need to protect the locals.
Henry	And the Stapletons!
Watson	The man is a danger to the community with his brutal and violent nature. I will come too. I have my revolver. Are you armed?
Henry	I have a hunting-crop.
Watson	We shall take him by surprise and have him at our mercy before he can resist.
Henry	I say, Watson, what would Holmes say to this?
Watson	He'd say that this is the hour of darkness in which the power of evil is exalted!

Act 2 Scene 5 The Moor (Night)

(Sound of wind and strange cry/howl, vibrating through the auditorium.)

Henry   My God, what's that, Watson, was it the cry of a hound? *(His voice breaking.)*

Watson   The folk on the countryside say it is the cry of the Hound of the Baskervilles.

Henry   A hound it was, but it seemed to come from miles away, over yonder, I think. It was up there at Grimpen Mire. Come now, Watson, don't you think it was the cry of a hound?

Watson   Stapleton was with me when I heard it last. He said that it might be the calling of a strange bird.

Henry   No, no, it was a hound. My God, can there be some truth in all these stories? Is it possible that I am really in danger from so dark a cause? You don't believe it, do you, Watson?

Watson   No, no.

Henry   Oh my poor uncle! There was the footprint of the hound beside him where he lay. It all fits together. I don't think that I am a coward, Watson, but that sound seemed to freeze my very blood. Feel my hand.

Watson   It's freezing.

Henry   I don't think I'll get that cry out of my head. What do you advise that we do now?

Watson   Shall we turn back?

Henry   No, by thunder; we have come out to get our man, and we will do it. Come on! We'll see it through even if all the fiends of the pit were loose upon the moor. There's his lantern. What shall we do now?

Watson   Wait here. He must be near his light. Let us see if we can get a glimpse of him.

Henry   There he is.

(We see Selden, filthy, bearded, long hair. He sees Henry and Watson and attacks them. There is a fight and chase as realistic as possible on the stage then around the auditorium, if possible. During the struggle the revolver goes off by mistake. Selden gets away and runs off. Henry watches after him.)

Watson   *(Gun shot.)* Heavens my gun. I only brought it with me for self-defence. I never....We must warn the people of Princetown.

(He looks up and stops. Silence and then we see a tall dark figure at the back of the stage. The blacks will open making the stage bigger and emptier. Music getting louder. He should be standing high up, totally still with a strong light behind him, like the moon, putting him into silhouette. His clothes are tailored and he wears a hat. It should obviously not be Selden. He stands for a few seconds then disappears.)

Watson   *(Stunned.)* Did you see him?

Henry   Not really.

Watson   There are two men on the moor. Could that have been our man in the Hansom Cab in London?

Henry   That damned stranger is still dogging us here as he did in London.

Watson   I fear we have never shaken him off. If I could lay my hands on that man then... Where did he go?

Henry   Watson, first we must warn the police that Selden is still on the run.

Barrymore   *(Over hearing as he runs on.)* I heard the shot, what happened?

Watson   He's run off, no harm done, we didn't get him.

Barrymore   *(Furious.)* It is unfair on your part to hunt my brother-in-law down when I told you about him in confidence. The poor fellow has enough to fight against without my putting more upon his track.

Henry   If you had told us of your own free will it would have been different but you only told us, or rather your wife only told us, when it was forced from you and you could not help yourself.

Barrymore   I didn't think you would have taken advantage of it, Sir Henry, indeed I didn't.

Watson   The man is a public danger. There are lonely houses scattered over the moor, Look at Mr. Stapleton's house, for example, with no one but himself to defend it. There's no safety for anyone until he is under lock and key.

Barrymore   He'll break into no house, sir. I give you my solemn word upon that. I assure you, Sir Henry, that in a very few days the necessary arrangements will have been made and he will be on his way to South America. For God's sake, sir, I beg of you not to let the police know that he is still on the moor. They have given up the chase there, and he can lie quiet until the ship is ready for him. You can't tell on him without getting my wife and I into trouble. I beg you, sir, to say nothing to the police.

Henry   What do you say, Watson?

Watson   If he were safely out of the country it would relieve the tax-payer of a burden.

Henry	But how about the chance of his holding someone up before he goes?
Barrymore	He would not do anything so mad, sir. We have provided him with all that he can want. To commit a crime would be to show where he was hiding.
Henry	That is true...Well, Barrymore –
Barrymore	God bless you, sir, and thank you from my heart! It would have killed my poor wife had he been taken again.
Henry	I guess we are aiding and abetting a felony, Watson? But, after what we have heard I don't feel as if I could give the man up, so there is an end of it. All right, Barrymore, you can go.
Barrymore	You've been so kind to us, sir, that I should like to do the best I can for you in return. I know something, Sir Henry, and perhaps I should have said it before, but it was long after the inquest that I found it out. I've never breathed a word about it yet to mortal man. It's about poor Sir Charles's death.
Henry	Do you know how he died?
Barrymore	No, sir, I don't, I know why he was at the gate at that hour. It was to meet a woman.
Watson	To meet a woman! He?
Barrymore	Yes, sir.
Watson	And the woman's name?
Barrymore	I can't give you the name, sir, but I can give you the initials. Her initials were L. L.
Henry	How do you know this, Barrymore?
Barrymore	Well, Sir Henry, as it chanced, there was only one letter that morning, so I took the more notice of it. It was from Coombe Tracey, and it was addressed in a woman's hand.
Watson	Well?
Barrymore	Well, sir, I thought no more of the matter, and never would have done had it not been for my wife. Only a few weeks ago she was cleaning out Sir Charles's study - it had never been touched since his death - and she found the ashes of a burned letter in the back of the grate, one little slip, the end of a page, hung together, and the writing could still be read. It seemed to us to be a postscript at the end of the letter and it said: ' Please, please, as you are a gentleman, burn this letter, and be at the gate by ten o'clock. Beneath it were signed the initials L. L.

Watson	*(Making a note in his notebook)* Have you got that slip?
Barrymore	No, sir, it crumbled all to bits after we moved it.
Watson	Had Sir Charles received any other letters in the same writing?
Barrymore	Well, sir, I took no particular notice of his letters. I should not have noticed this one, only it happened to come alone.
Henry	And you have no idea who L. L. is?
Barrymore	No, sir. No more than you have. But I expect if we could lay our hands upon that lady we should know more about Sir Charles's death.
Henry	I cannot understand, Barrymore, how you came to conceal this important information.
Barrymore	Well, sir, it was immediately after that our own trouble came to us. We were both of us very fond of Sir Charles, to rake this up couldn't help our poor master, and it is well to go carefully when there's a lady in the case. Even the best of us -
Watson	You thought it might injure his reputation?
Barrymore	Well, sir, I thought no good could come of it. But now you have been kind to us, and I feel as if it would be treating you unfairly not to tell you all that I know about the matter.
Henry	Very good, Barrymore; you can go. Well, Watson, what do you think of this new information?
Watson	It seems to leave the darkness rather blacker than before.
Barrymore	I'm so sorry to interrupt Sir, but that other light on the moor is probably the other man living on the moor.
Watson	You know about the other man? How do you know of him then?
Barrymore	Selden told me of him, sir, a week ago or more. He's in hiding, too, but he's not a convict as far as I can make out. I don't like it, Dr. Watson -- I tell you straight, sir, that I don't like it. *(Passionately.)*
Watson	Tell me, frankly, what it is that you don't like.
Barrymore	It's all these goings-on, sir. There's foul play somewhere, and there's black villainy brewing, to that I'll swear! Very glad I should be, sir, to see Sir Henry on his way back to London again!
Henry	But what is it that alarms you?

Barrymore	Look at Sir Charles's death! That was bad enough. Look at the noises on the moor at night. There's not a man would cross it after sundown if he was paid for it. Look at this stranger hiding out yonder, and watching and waiting! What's he waiting for? What does it mean? It means no good to anyone of the name of Baskerville, and very glad I shall be to be quit of it all on the day that Sir Henry's new servants are ready to take over the Hall.
Watson	But about this stranger. Can you tell me anything about him? What did Selden say? Did he find out where he hid, or what he was doing?
Barrymore	He saw him once or twice, but he is a deep one and gives nothing away. At first he thought that he was the police. A kind of gentleman he was, as far as he could see, but what he was doing he could not make out.
Watson	And where did he say that he lived?
Barrymore	Among the old houses on the hillside - the stone huts where the ancient folk used to live.
Henry	But how about his food?
Barrymore	Selden found out that he has got a lad who works for him and brings all he needs. I dare say he goes to Coombe Tracey for what he wants.
Henry	Very good, Barrymore. Thank you.
Barrymore	My pleasure Sir. *(Exits.)*
Watson	So things are coming together fast now. What passion of hatred can it be which leads a man to lurk in such a place at such a time! And what deep and earnest purpose can he have which calls for such a trial! In that hut upon the moor, seems to lie the very centre of that problem which has vexed us so sorely. I swear that another day shall not have passed before we have done all that man can do to reach the heart of the mystery.
Henry	Now if we can only trace L. L. it should clear up the whole business. We have gained that much. We know that there is someone who has the facts if we can only find her. What do you think we should do?
Watson	I only wish Holmes were here.
Mortimer	*(Entering.)* I got here as quickly as I could, is anyone hurt?
Watson	We were chasing that wretched prisoner Selden and my revolver went off by mistake. Dr Mortimer you got here surprisingly quickly, your house is four miles away.
Mortimer	I was on the moor searching for my mastiff, he wandered off hours ago. I fear he may have gone close to Grimpen Mire, God forbid.

Watson	If I could keep you for one minute Doctor...I suppose there are few people living within driving distance of here whom you do not know?
Mortimer	Hardly any, I think.
Watson	Can you tell me then of any woman whose initials are L. L.?
Mortimer	I can't think straight...Wait a bit though, there is Laura Lyons - her initials are L. L. -but she lives in Coombe Tracey.
Watson	Who is she?
Mortimer	She is Frankland's daughter.
Henry	What! Old Frankland the crank?
Mortimer	Exactly. She married an artist named Lyons, who came sketching on the moor. He proved to be a blackguard and deserted her. Her father refused to have anything to do with her because she had married without his consent and then proceeded to divorce him! So, between the old sinner and the young one the woman has had a pretty bad time.
Watson	How does she live?
Mortimer	I fancy old Frankland allows her a pittance. Her story got about, and several of the people here did something to enable her to earn an honest living. Stapleton did for one, and Sir Charles for another. I gave a trifle myself. It was to set her up in a typewriting business. I really must continue my search. *(Runs off.)*
Watson	Sir Henry, I suggest we go home now. Make sure Barrymore has checked all the windows and doors and have a good night's sleep. Tomorrow is another day and I shall go and visit this lady Laura Lyons. I shall go alone to make it less formal.

Act 2 Scene 6 Laura Lyons' Abode

(Scene set down stage right Right.)

Watson	I have the pleasure of knowing your father, Mrs Lyons. My name is Dr Watson.
Laura	I have heard of you Dr. Watson, however, there is nothing in common between my father and me. I owe him nothing. If it were not for the late Sir Charles Baskerville and some other kind hearts I might have starved for all that my father cared.
Watson	It was about the late Sir Charles Baskerville that I have come here to see you.
Laura	What can I tell you about him? *(Nervous.)*
Watson	You knew him, did you not?
Laura	I have already said that I owe a great deal to his kindness. If I am able to support myself it is largely due to the interest which he took in my unhappy situation.
Watson	Did you correspond with him?
Laura	What is the object of these questions?
Watson	The object is to avoid a public scandal. It is better that I should ask them here than that the matter should pass outside our control.
Laura	Well, I'll answer. What are your questions?
Watson	Did you correspond with Sir Charles?
Laura	I certainly wrote to him once or twice to acknowledge his delicacy and his generosity.
Watson	Have you the dates of those letters?
Laura	No.
Watson	Have you ever met him?
Laura	Yes, once or twice, when he came into Coombe Tracey.
Watson	But if you saw him so seldom and wrote so seldom, how did he know enough about your affairs to be able to help you, as you say that he has done?
Laura	There were several who knew my sad history and united to help me. One was Mr. Stapleton, a neighbour and intimate friend of Sir Charles's. He was

59

	exceedingly kind, and it was through him that Sir Charles learned about my affairs.
Watson	Did you ever write to Sir Charles asking him to meet you?
Laura	Really, sir, this is a very extraordinary question.
Watson	I am sorry, madam, but I must repeat it.
Laura	Then I answer, certainly not!
Watson	Not on the very day of Sir Charles's death?
Laura	No
Watson	Surely your memory deceives you. I quote, *(reading from his notebook)* 'Please, please, as you are a gentleman, burn this letter, and be at the gate by ten o'clock.'
Laura	Is there no such thing as a gentleman?
Watson	Ah, but he did burn the letter. Sometimes a letter may be legible even when burned. You acknowledge now that you wrote it?
Laura	Yes, I did write it, I did write it. Why should I deny it? I have no reason to be ashamed of it. I wished him to help me. I believed that if I had an interview I could gain his help, so I asked him to meet me.
Watson	But why at such an hour?
Laura	Because I had only just learned that he was going to London next day and might be away for months. There were reasons why I could not get there earlier.
Watson	But why a rendezvous in the garden instead of a visit to the house?
Laura	Do you think a woman could go alone at that hour to a bachelor's house?
Watson	Well, what happened when you did get there?
Laura	I never went.
Watson	Mrs. Lyons!
Laura	No, I swear it to you on all I hold sacred. I never went. Something intervened to prevent my going.
Watson	What was that?
Laura	That is a private matter. I cannot tell it.

Watson	You acknowledge then that you made an appointment with Sir Charles at the very hour and place at which he met his death, but you deny keeping the appointment. What is the truth?... Mrs. Lyons, if I have to call in the aid of the police you will find how seriously you are compromised. If your position is innocent, why did you in the first instance deny having written to Sir Charles upon that date?
Laura	Because I feared that some false conclusion might be drawn from it and that I might find myself involved in a scandal.
Watson	And why were you so pressing that Sir Charles should destroy your letter?
Laura	If you have read the letter you will know.
Watson	I did not say that I had read all the letter. I merely quoted the postscript. The letter had, as I said, been burned and it was not all legible. I ask you once again why it was that you were so pressing that Sir Charles should destroy this letter which he received on the very day of his death.
Laura	The matter is a very private one.
Watson	The more reason why you should avoid a public investigation.
Laura	I made a rash marriage and had reason to regret it. My life has been one incessant persecution from a husband whom I abhor. The law is upon his side, and every day I am faced by the possibility that he may force me to live with him. At the time that I wrote this letter to Sir Charles I had learned that there was a prospect of my regaining my freedom if certain expenses could be met. It meant everything to me - peace of mind, happiness, self-respect - everything. I knew Sir Charles's generosity, and I thought that if he heard the story from my own lips he would help me.
Watson	Then how is it that you did not go?
Laura	Because I received help in the interval from another source.
Watson	Then, did you not write to Sir Charles and explain this?
Laura	So I should have done had I not seen his death in the paper next morning.
Watson	Thank you, Mrs Lyons. I am aware that you had instituted divorce proceedings against your husband at about the time of the tragedy so, thank you for your patience and for being so candid. Goodbye.
Laura	Good day Dr Watson.

Act 2 Scene 7 The Moor (Daylight)

Watson *(To audience.)* I had not gone far when I heard someone running behind me. I turned around to see Dr Mortimer. She was flushed and obviously tired. Doctor any sign of your dog yet? It must have been missing for about 24 hours now.

Mortimer No Dr. Watson I started my hunt again at sunrise. I fear the worst. The moor is even more treacherous at night. I saw you in the distance and thought I'd tell you something Frankland told me when I was up near his house searching. I asked him if he'd seen my dog through his telescope on his roof, he told me no, but he'd seen a young urchin every day at the same time climbing up, furtively with a bundle over his shoulder towards the pre-historic huts on The Tor. It is his belief he was taking food to someone in hiding up there.

Watson (To Audience.) I thanked the doctor and wished her luck, believing it was by now far too late for her beloved dog to be found alive. The sun was already sinking when I reached the summit of the hill. The barren scene, the sense of loneliness, and the mystery and urgency of my task all struck a chill into my heart. In a cleft of the hills there was a circle of the old stone huts and in the middle was one which retained sufficient roof to act as a screen against the weather. My heart leaped as I saw it. This must be the burrow where the stranger lurked. My nerves tingled with the sense of adventure.

Throwing aside my cigarette, I closed my hand upon the butt of my revolver and, walking swiftly up to the door, I looked in. The place was empty apart from a loaf of bread and, next to it, a sheet of paper with writing upon it. "Dr. Watson has gone to Coombe Tracey." It was I, then, and not Sir Henry, who was being dogged by this secret man. I swore that I would not leave the hut until he returned. I'm not ashamed to admit my heart felt as if it would burst.

Holmes It is a lovely evening, my dear Watson. *(He is perfectly dressed.)*

Watson Holmes! Holmes!

Holmes Come out, and please be careful with the revolver.

Watson I never was more glad to see anyone in my life.

Holmes The surprise was not all on one side, I assure you. I had no idea that you had found my occasional retreat until I was within twenty paces of the door.

Watson My footprint, I presume?

Holmes No, Watson, I fear that I could not undertake to recognize your footprint amid all the footprints of the world. If you seriously desire to deceive me you must change your tobacconist; for when I see the stub of a cigarette marked Bradley, Oxford Street, I know that my friend Watson is in the neighbourhood. So you actually thought that I was the criminal?

Watson	I did not know who you were, but I was determined to find out.
Holmes	Excellent, Watson! And how did you localize me? You saw me, perhaps, on the night of the convict hunt, when I was so imprudent as to allow the moon to rise behind me?
Watson	Yes, I saw you then and your boy had been observed, and that gave me a guide where to look.
Holmes	The old gentleman with the telescope, no doubt. I could not make it out when first I saw the light flashing upon the lens. Ha, I see that Cartwright has brought up some supplies. What's this note? So you have been to Coombe Tracey, have you, to see Mrs. Laura Lyons?
Watson	Exactly.
Holmes	Well done! Our researches have evidently been running on parallel lines, and when we unite our results I expect we shall have a fairly full knowledge of the case.
Watson	Well, I am glad from my heart that you are here, for indeed the responsibility and the mystery were both becoming too much for my nerves. But how in the name of wonder did you come here, and what have you been doing? I thought that you were back in Baker Street working out that case of blackmailing.
Holmes	That was what I wished you to think.
Watson	Then you use me, and yet do not trust me! *(Bitter.)* I think that I have deserved better at your hands, Holmes.
Holmes	My dear fellow, you have been invaluable to me in this as in many other cases, and I beg that you will forgive me if I have seemed to play a trick upon you. In truth, it was partly for your own sake that I did it, and it was my appreciation of the danger which you ran which led me to come down and examine the matter for myself. Had I been with Sir Henry and you it is confident that my point of view would have been the same as yours, and my presence would have warned our very formidable opponents to be on their guard. As it is, I have been able to get about as I could not possibly have done had I been living in the Hall, and I remain an unknown factor in the business, ready to throw in all my weight at a critical moment.
Watson	But why keep me in the dark?
Holmes	For you to know could not have helped us and might possibly have led to my discovery. You would have wished to tell me something, or in your kindness you would have brought me out some comfort or other, and so an unnecessary risk would be run. I brought Cartwright down with me - you remember the little chap at the express office? And he has seen after my simple wants: a loaf of bread and a clean collar. What does man want more? He has given me an

extra pair of eyes upon a very active pair of feet, and both have been invaluable.

Watson   Then my reports have all been wasted! *(Annoyed.)*

Holmes   Here are your reports, my dear fellow, and very well thumbed, I assure you. I must compliment you exceedingly upon the zeal and the intelligence which you have shown over an extraordinarily difficult case. *(Watson smiles.)*...That's better, and now tell me the result of your visit to Mrs. Laura Lyons.

Watson   Here are my notes. *(Shows his notebook to Holmes.)*

Holmes   This is most important, it fills up a gap which I had been unable to bridge in this most complex affair. You are aware, perhaps, that a close intimacy exists between this lady and the man Stapleton?

Watson   I did not know of a close intimacy.

Holmes   There can be no doubt about the matter. They meet, they write, there is a complete understanding between them. Now, this puts a very powerful weapon into our hands. If I could only use it to detach his wife

Watson   His wife?

Holmes   The lady who has passed here as Miss Stapleton is in reality his wife.

Watson   Good heavens, Holmes! Are you sure of what you say? How could he have permitted Sir Henry to fall in love with her?

Holmes   Sir Henry's falling in love could do no harm to anyone except Sir Henry. He took particular care that Sir Henry did not make love to her, as you have yourself observed. I repeat that the lady is his wife and not his sister.

Watson   But why this elaborate deception?

Holmes   Because he foresaw that she would be very much more useful to him in the character of a free woman.

Watson   I saw an impassive colourless man, with his straw hat and his butterfly-net, but now I see something terrible - a creature of infinite patience and craft, with a smiling face and a murderous heart. It is he who is our enemy. Is it he who dogged us in London?

Holmes   So I read the riddle.

Watson   And the warning - it must have come from Maria!

Holmes   Exactly.

Watson	But are you sure of this, Holmes? How can you be certain that the woman is his wife?
Holmes	Because he so far forgot himself as to tell you a true piece of autobiography upon the occasion when he first met you, and I dare say he has many a time regretted it since. He was once a schoolmaster in the north of England. Now, there is no one more easy to trace than a schoolmaster. A little investigation showed me that a school had come to grief under atrocious circumstances, and that the man who had owned it - the name was different - had disappeared with his wife. The descriptions agreed. When I learned that the missing man was devoted to entomology the identification was complete.
Watson	If this woman is in truth his wife, where does Mrs. Laura Lyons come in?
Holmes	That is one of the points upon which your own researches have shed a light. Your interview with the lady has cleared the situation very much. I did not know about a projected divorce between herself and her husband. In that case, regarding Stapleton as an unmarried man, she counted no doubt upon becoming his wife.
Watson	And when she is undeceived?
Holmes	Why, then we may find the lady of service. It must be our first duty to see her - both of us - to-morrow. Don't you think Watson that you are away from your charge rather long? Your place should be at Baskerville Hall.
Watson	One last question, Holmes, surely there is no need of secrecy between you and me. What is the meaning of it all? What is he after?
Holmes	It is murder, Watson - refined, cold-blooded, deliberate murder. Do not ask me for particulars. My nets are closing upon him, even as his are upon Sir Henry, and with your help he is already almost at my mercy. There is but one danger which can threaten us. It is that he should strike before we are ready to do so. Another day - two at the most - and I have my case complete, but until then guard your charge as closely as ever a fond mother watched her ailing child. Your mission to-day has justified itself, and yet I could almost wish that you had not left his side. *(A terrible scream.)* Hark!
Watson	Oh, my God! What is it? What does it mean?
Holmes	Hush! Hush! *(The cry is coming closer.)* Where is it? Where is it, Watson?
Watson	There, I think*! (Cry again.)*
Holmes	No, there it is again
Watson	The hound. Great heavens, if we are too late!
Holmes	(Starting to run.) He has beaten us, Watson. We are too late.

Watson	No, no, surely not!
Holmes	Fool that I was to hold my hand. And you, Watson, see what comes of abandoning your charge! But, by Heaven, if the worst has happened we'll avenge him.
Watson	What can you see?
Holmes	It's the body of Sir Henry Baskerville! In his sheepskin jacket.
Watson	The brute! The brute! Oh Holmes, I shall never forgive myself for having left him to his fate.
Holmes	I am more to blame than you, Watson. In order to have my case well rounded and complete, I have thrown away the life of my client. It is the greatest blow which has befallen me in my career. But how could I know - how could I know - that he would risk his life alone upon the moor in the face of all my warnings?
Watson	Where is this brute of a hound which drove him to his death? And Stapleton, where is he? He shall answer for this deed.
Holmes	He shall. I will see to that. Uncle and nephew have been murdered - the one frightened to death by the very sight of a beast which he thought to be supernatural, the other driven to his end in his wild flight to escape from it. But now we have to prove the connection between the man and the beast. Apart from what we heard, we cannot even swear to the existence of the latter, since Sir Henry has evidently died from the fall. But, cunning as he is, the fellow shall be in my power before another day is past!

(They climb a hill, if they can, or move upstage.)

Watson	I can see his light. Why should we not seize him at once?
Holmes	Our case is not complete. The fellow is wary and cunning to the last degree. It is not what we know, but what we can prove. If we make one false move the villain may escape us yet.
Watson	What can we do?
Holmes	There will be plenty for us to do to-morrow. To-night we can only perform the last offices to our poor friend.
Watson	We must send for help, Holmes! *(Holmes is turning the body over.)* We cannot carry him all the way to the Hall. Good heavens, are you mad?
Holmes	A beard! A beard! The man has a beard! *(Laughing.)*
Watson	A beard?

Holmes	It is not the baronet... it is...why, it is my neighbour, the convict! Selden.
Watson	Barrymore passed on Sir Henry's clothes in order to help Selden in his escape.
Holmes	Then the clothes have been the poor devil's death. It is clear enough that the hound has been laid on from some article of Sir Henry's. The boot which was abstracted in the hotel, in all probability, and so ran this man down. There is one very singular thing, however: how came Selden, in the darkness, to know that the hound was on his trail?
Watson	He heard him.
Holmes	To hear a hound upon the moor would not work a hard man like this convict into such a paroxysm of terror that he would risk recapture by screaming wildly for help. By his cries he must have run a long way after he knew the animal was on his track. How did he know?
Watson	A greater mystery to me is why this hound, presuming that all our conjectures are correct -
Holmes	I presume nothing.
Watson	Well, then, why this hound should be loose to-night. Stapleton would not let it go unless he had reason to think that Sir Henry would be there.
Holmes	My difficulty is the more formidable of the two, for I think that we shall very shortly get an explanation of yours, while mine may remain forever a mystery. The question now is, what shall we do with this poor wretch's body? We cannot leave it here to the foxes and the ravens?
Watson	I suggest that we put it in one of the huts until we can communicate with the police.
Holmes	Exactly. I have no doubt that you and I could carry it so far. Quiet, Watson. It's the man himself. Not a word to show your suspicions, not a word, or my plans crumble to the ground.
	(Enter Stapleton.)
Stapleton	Why, Dr. Watson, that's not you, is it? You are the last man that I should have expected to see out on the moor at this time of night. But, dear me, what's this? Somebody hurt? Not? Don't tell me that it is our friend Sir Henry*! (Sharp intake of his breath.)*...Who, who's this?
Watson	It is Selden, the man who escaped from Princetown.
Stapleton	Dear me! What a very shocking affair! How did he die?
Holmes	He appears to have broken his neck by falling over these rocks. My friend and I were strolling on the moor when we heard a cry.

Stapleton	I heard a cry also. That was what brought me out. I was uneasy about Sir Henry.
Watson	Why about Sir Henry in particular?
Stapleton	Because I had suggested that he should come over. When he did not come I was surprised, and I naturally became alarmed for his safety when I heard cries upon the moor. By the way did you hear anything else besides a cry?
Holmes	No, did you?
Stapleton	No.
Holmes	What do you mean, then?
Stapleton	Oh, you know the stories that the peasants tell about a phantom hound, and so on. It is said to be heard at night upon the moor. I was wondering if there were any evidence of such a sound to-night.
Watson	We heard nothing of the kind.
Stapleton	And what is your theory of this poor fellow's death?
Watson	I have no doubt that anxiety and exposure have driven him off his head. He has rushed about the moor in a crazy state and eventually fallen over here and broken his neck.
Stapleton	That seems the most reasonable theory. *(Sigh of relief.)* What do you think about it, Mr. Sherlock Holmes?
Holmes	You are quick at identification.
Stapleton	We have been expecting you in these parts since Dr. Watson came down. You are in time to see a tragedy.
Holmes	Yes, indeed. I have no doubt that my friend's explanation will cover the facts. I will take an unpleasant remembrance back to London with me to-morrow.
Stapleton	Oh, you return to-morrow?
Holmes	That is my intention.
Stapleton	I hope your visit has cast some light upon those occurrences which have puzzled us?
Holmes	One cannot always have the success for which one hopes. An investigator needs facts and not legends or rumours. It has not been a satisfactory case.

Stapleton	I would suggest carrying this poor fellow to my house, but it would give my sister such a fright that I do not feel justified in doing it. I think that he will be safe here until morning. *(Exit.)*
Holmes	We're at close grips at last. What a nerve the fellow has! It must have been a paralyzing shock when he found that the wrong man had fallen a victim to his plot. I told you in London, Watson, and I tell you now again, that we have never had a foeman more worthy of our steel.
Watson	Why should we not arrest him at once?
Holmes	My dear Watson, you were born to be a man of action. Your instinct is always to do something energetic. But supposing, for argument's sake, that we had him arrested to-night? We could prove nothing against him. There's the devilish cunning of it! If he were acting through a human agent we could get some evidence, but if we were to drag this great dog to the light of day it would not help us in putting a rope round the neck of its master.
Watson	Surely we have a case.
Holmes	Not a shadow of one; only surmise and conjecture. We should be laughed out of court if we came with such a story and such evidence.
Watson	There is Sir Charles's death.
Holmes	Found dead without a mark upon him. You and I know that he died of sheer fright, and we know also what frightened him, but how are we to get twelve stolid jurymen to know it? What signs are there of a hound? Where are the marks of its fangs? Of course we know that a hound does not bite a dead body and that Sir Charles was dead before ever the brute overtook him.
Watson	Well, then, to-night?
Holmes	We are not much better off to-night. Again, there was no direct connection between the hound and the man's death. No, my dear fellow; we must reconcile ourselves to the fact that we have no case at present, and that it is worth our while to run any risk in order to establish one.
Watson	And how do you propose to do so?
Holmes	I have great hopes of what Mrs. Laura Lyons may do for us when the position of affairs is made clear to her. And I have my own plan as well. I hope before tomorrow is past to have the upper hand at last.
Watson	Are you coming in?
Holmes	Yes; I see no reason for further concealment. But one last word, Watson. Say nothing of the hound to Sir Henry. Let him think that Selden's death was as Stapleton would have us believe. If I remember your report aright, he is to dine with these people.

Watson   And so am I.

Holmes   Then you must excuse yourself and he must go alone. That will be easily
              arranged. Let's go in. *(Lights up to depict part of Hall across downstage area
              so as not to have to reset the whole Hall.)*

Act 2 Scene 8 Baskerville Hall

Watson	*(To the audience.)* Sir Henry was more pleased than surprised to see Sherlock Holmes, for he had for some days been expecting that recent events would bring him down from London. We explained to the baronet as much of our experience as it seemed desirable that he should know, but first I had the unpleasant duty of breaking the news to Barrymore and his wife. To him it may have been an unmitigated relief, but she wept bitterly into her apron. To all the world Selden was the man of violence, half animal and half demon; but to her he always remained the little boy who had clung to her hand. Evil indeed is the man who has not one woman to mourn him.
Henry	If I hadn't sworn not to go about alone I might have had a more lively evening, for I had a message from Stapleton asking me over there.
Holmes	I have no doubt that you would have had a more lively evening. By the way, I don't suppose you appreciate that we have been mourning over you as having broken your neck?
Henry	How was that?
Holmes	Selden was dressed in your clothes. I fear your servant who gave them to him may get into trouble with the police.
Henry	That is unlikely. There was no mark of ownership on any of them, as far as I know. How are you coming along with the case.
Holmes	*(Walking along front of stage, a channel of light creating the image that he is looking at the portraits .)* I think that I shall be in a position to make the situation rather more clear to you before long. It has been an exceedingly difficult and most complicated business. There are several points upon which we still want light -- but it is coming all the same if you will give me your help... without always asking the reason.
Henry	Whatever you tell me to do I will do.
Holmes	*(Stops suddenly staring at a portrait.)* They are all family portraits, I presume? Who is this?
Henry	He is the cause of all the mischief, the wicked Hugo, who started the Hound of the Baskervilles. We're not likely to forget him.
Holmes	Dear me! He seems a quiet, meek-mannered man enough, but I dare say that there was a lurking devil in his eyes. *(Aside to Watson.)* Do you see anything there?
Watson	Good heavens! It might be a portrait of Stapleton!
Holmes	The fellow is a Baskerville. That is evident.

Watson	With designs upon the succession.
Holmes	Exactly. We have him, Watson, we have him, and I dare swear that before to-morrow night he will be fluttering in our net as helpless as one of his own butterflies. *(To Henry.)* You are engaged, as I understand, to dine with our friends the Stapletons tomorrow?
Henry	I hope that you will come also.
Holmes	I fear that Watson and I must go to London.
Henry	To London?
Holmes	Yes, I think that we should be more useful there at the present juncture.
Henry	I hoped that you were going to see me through this business. The Hall and the moor are not very pleasant places when one is alone.
Holmes	My dear fellow, you must trust me implicitly and do exactly what I tell you. You can tell your friends that we should have been happy to have come with you, but that urgent business required us to be in town. We hope very soon to return to Devonshire. Will you remember to give them that message?
Henry	If you insist upon it.
Holmes	There is no alternative, I assure you.
Henry	When do you desire to go?
Holmes	Early afternoon. We will drive in to Coombe Tracey, but Watson will leave his things as a pledge that he will come back to you. Watson, you will send a note to Stapleton to tell him that you regret that you cannot come. One more direction Sir Henry! I wish you to drive to Merripit House, send back your trap, however, and let them know that you intend to walk home.
Henry	To walk across the moor?
Holmes	Yes.
Henry	But that is the very thing which you have so often cautioned me not to do.
Holmes	This time you may do it with safety. If I had not every confidence in your nerve and courage I would not suggest it, but it is essential that you should do it.
Henry	Then I will do it.
Holmes	And as you value your life do not go across the moor in any direction save along the straight path which leads from Merripit House to the Grimpen Road, and is your natural way home.

Henry	I will do just what you say. *(He exits)*
Holmes	*(To Henry as he goes)* Very good. I should be glad to get away by 1, so as to reach London in the early evening.
Watson	*(Aside to Holmes.)* I cannot help saying I am astounded. I do not understand why we will both be absent at the moment which you say is critical.
Holmes	Never question my motives Watson, never. What we really will do is pay a visit to Mrs Lyons and never be far from Sir Henry.

Act 2 Scene 9 Laura Lyons' Abode

(Black out scene change, lights up SL Laura Lyons house SR.)

Holmes	*(They walk stage left.)* Good afternoon to you. I am investigating the circumstances which attended the death of the late Sir Charles Baskerville. My friend here, Dr. Watson, has informed me of what you have communicated, and also of what you have withheld in connection with that matter.
Laura	What have I withheld? *(Defiantly.)*
Holmes	You have confessed that you asked Sir Charles to be at the gate at ten o'clock. We know that that was the place and hour of his death. You have withheld what the connection is between these events.
Laura	There is no connection.
Holmes	In that case the coincidence must indeed be an extraordinary one. But I think that we shall succeed in establishing a connection, after all. I wish to be perfectly frank with you, Mrs. Lyons. We regard this case as one of murder, and the evidence may implicate not only your friend Mr. Stapleton but his wife as well.
Laura	His wife!
Holmes	The fact is no longer a secret. The person who has passed for his sister is really his wife.
Laura	His wife! His wife! He is not a married man. I know him. He is not married.
Holmes	Indeed he is.
Laura	Mr Holmes, or whatever your name is, you are mistaken. Jack Stapleton is not married and never has been I am sure of it. I know him.
Holmes	Madam I have a copy of his wedding certificate, dated 1896, between him and Maria.
Laura	Let me see that, it must be a forgery, a fake. Is this some kind of trick or joke? This man offered me marriage on condition that I could get a divorce from my husband. I want more proof, why should I believe a total stranger? Tell me that. Why?
Holmes	I have come prepared. Here is a wedding photograph of the couple taken in York five years ago. You will see they are in wedding attire and before you question that here is an announcement in the newspaper. No doubt about it.
Laura	He has lied to me, the villain, in every conceivable way. Not one word of truth has he ever told me. And why? Why? I see that I was never anything but a

	tool in his hands. Why should I try to shield him from the consequences of his own wicked acts? Ask me what you like, and there is nothing which I shall hold back. One thing I swear to you, and that is that when I wrote the letter I never dreamed of any harm to the old gentleman, who had been my kindest friend.
Holmes	This must be very painful to you; perhaps it will make it easier if I tell you what occurred, and you can check me if I make any material mistake. The sending of this letter was suggested to you by Stapleton?
Laura	*(Slight hesitation.)* He dictated it.
Holmes	I presume that the reason he gave was that you would receive help from Sir Charles for the legal expenses connected with your divorce?
Laura	Exactly.
Holmes	And then after you had sent the letter he dissuaded you from keeping the appointment?
Laura	He told me that it would hurt his self-respect that any other man should find the money for such an object, and that though he was a poor man himself he would devote his last penny to removing the obstacles which divided us.
Holmes	He appears to be a very consistent character. And then you heard nothing until you read the reports of the death in the paper?
Laura	No.
Holmes	And he made you swear to say nothing about your appointment with Sir Charles?
Laura	He did. He said that the death was a very mysterious one, and that I should certainly be suspected if the facts came out. He frightened me into remaining silent.
Holmes	Quite so. But you had your suspicions? I think that on the whole you have had a fortunate escape. You are alive. We must wish you good day now, Mrs. Lyons, and it is probable that you will very shortly hear from us again.

Act 2 Scene 10 The Moor (dusk)

(They leave her house, stage getting darker as they walk.)

Holmes   Our case becomes rounded off, and difficulty after difficulty thins away in front of us. I shall soon be in the position of being able to put into a single connected narrative one of the most singular and sensational crimes of modern times. Even now we have no clear case against this very wily man. Now it's a waiting game.

Watson   Holmes you are maddening, you never reveal what you are up to. That's Merripit House just up ahead.

Holmes   The end of our journey. I must request you to walk on tiptoe and not to talk above a whisper.

(They tip toe a little further.)

Holmes   We shall make our little ambush here. Creep forward quietly and see what they are doing, but for heaven's sake don't let them know that they are watched!

Watson   I can only see Stapleton and Sir Henry. Maria is not there. Sir Henry is looking very pale. Perhaps it's the thought of the lonely walk back to The Hall. Stapleton has just come out to look in the outhouse. He's unlocked the door, looked in there, locked it up again and is returning to the house.

Holmes   You say, Watson, that Maria is not there?

Watson   No. At least I cannot see her.

(Fog/smoke.)

Holmes   The Fog is moving towards us, Watson.

Watson   Is that serious?

Holmes   Very serious, indeed. The one thing upon earth which could have disarranged my plans. He can't be very long, now. It is already ten o'clock. Our success and even his life may depend upon his coming out before the fog is over the path... *(Puts his ear to the ground.)* Thank God, I think that I hear him coming.

Holmes   Hist! *(Click of pistol.)* Look out! It's coming! *(Hound's head appears centre between rocks, for only a split second.)*

Watson   *(Looking SR.)* Heavens Holmes it's the hound! It's enormous... its eyes.. I've never seen anything more hellish! *(Terrified.)*

(They both shoot at the Hound as if it's moved SR. Hideous howl.)

Watson	It's wounded. So it is mortal! Shoot Holmes. It's got Henry.
	(Hound roaring in pain.)
Holmes	It's down.
Henry	*(Stumbling on stage.)* My God! What was it? What, in heaven's name, was it?
Holmes	It's dead, whatever it is. We've laid the family ghost to rest once and for all.
Watson	It's enormous. The size of a lioness. Look it's covered in phosphorus. *(Wipes hand as if he's touched the hound.)*
Holmes	A cunning preparation of it. There is no smell which might have interfered with his power of scent. We owe you a deep apology, Sir Henry, for having exposed you to this fright. I was prepared for a hound, but not for such a creature as this. And the fog gave us little time to react.
Henry	You have saved my life.
Holmes	Having first endangered it. Are you strong enough to stand?
Henry	If you will help me up. I am fine. What do you propose to do?
Holmes	You are not fit for further adventures to-night. If you will wait, one or other of us will go back with you to the Hall. We must leave you now. We must get our man. Those shots must have told him that the game was up.
Watson	We were some distance off, and this fog may have deadened them.
Holmes	I'm certain he's gone by this time! But we'll search the house and make sure.
Watson	There's someone coming.
Maria	*(Running on.)* Is he safe? Has he escaped?
Watson	He cannot escape us, madam.
Maria	No, no, I did not mean my husband. Sir Henry, you are safe!
Henry	Yes.
Maria	And the hound?
Holmes	It is dead.
Maria	Thank God! Thank God! He tied me up in the outhouse! He hit me every time I refused to play his sordid game! It is my mind and soul that he has tortured and defiled. I tried so hard not to be involved with the hound. I could endure it all, ill-usage, solitude, a life of deception, everything, as long as I could still

cling to the hope that I had his love, but now I know that in this also I have been his dupe and his tool.(*Sobbing.*)

Holmes	Tell us then where we shall find him.
Maria	He'll go to the old tin mine on an island in the heart of the mire.
Holmes	No one could find his way into the Grimpen Mire to-night.
Maria	He may find his way in, but never out.
Henry	Come Maria, let's go back to Baskerville Hall together.
Maria	Please forgive me. I meant no harm. I tried to stop him. I tried to make you leave.
Henry	Of course I do. *(They exit.)*
Watson	And now I come rapidly to the conclusion of this most singular narrative. We gave chase into the foul quagmires which barred the way to any stranger. Rank reeds and lush, slimy water-plants sent an odour of decay and a heavy miasmatic vapour onto our faces. Holmes sank to his waist as he stepped from the path. *(Holmes and Watson 'carry out' this action until Holmes is safe, then Watson returns to his narrative).* Had I not been there to drag him out he could never have set his foot upon firm land again. He held an old black boot in the air.
Holmes	Meyers, Toronto. It is our friend Sir Henry's missing boot.
Watson	Thrown there by Stapleton in his flight.
Holmes	Exactly. He retained it in his hand after using it to set the hound upon the track. We know at least that he came so far in safety.
Watson	Holmes look there, the remains of a dog. We must be close to the mine now. Poor Dr Mortimer will never see her pet again. It must have been a meal for the hound.
Holmes	Hush, there are voices.

(Laura Lyons following Stapleton.)

Laura	You vile, evil devil, I trusted you, you adulterer. Without me you'd be nothing. How could you pretend for all those years your wife was your sister? Misleading me, making me think you wanted to marry me. You forget that it was I who found you and gave you the whole idea. Well I was only playing along with you because all I wanted was to become Lady Baskerville. I never loved you... Well this is where it ends!.. *(Pushes him down mine, depending on what can be achieved at each theatre. Use of a trap door or falls behind central fangs as if they are the mine.)*

Holmes	Mrs Lyons, stay right there. We heard and saw everything. We know you planned this together. You knew Sir Charles had a weak heart and planned that Jack would loose his hound on him. You used Maria as bait to gain Sir Henry's trust in Stapleton.
Laura	You're wrong about that, I had no idea she was his wife. *(Crying.)*
Holmes	That is the only true piece of information you have given me. You too recognised Stapleton for what he was, a Baskerville, but how did you track him down?
Laura	Why should I tell you?
Holmes	Because by confessing all now it may help you later, it may save you from the scaffold.
Laura	I didn't have to track him down. I saw his photograph in the newspaper in York. I recognised those evil features of Sir Hugo Baskerville. I'd seen them a hundred times on visits to Baskerville Hall with my father, as a child. A little research proved that I was right. He was the son of Roger Baskerville. He'd been adopted at a young age after his father's death and had a good claim on the fortune. I informed him he was the heir, but we had to keep it quiet. I told him about the old myth and together we sought out the largest dog we could possibly find and I discovered that phosphorus would make it look like a spectral hound. Jack promised to marry me once Sir Charles was out of the way and the estate was his, but then Sir Henry arrived from Canada. So I had to conjure up another plan, only this time the hound had to attack and kill. He told me he loved me, then you told me about his wife... He lied to me all that time, he's pulling me in... *(Screams.)* Help me! Help me! He's pulling me in. Help! *(Etc.)*

(We see her struggle as she is pulled down. Holmes and Watson try to save her...She's gone.)

Watson	Our attempts to help Laura Lyons were useless. Even during his own terror Jack had sought his revenge by dragging her down into the tin mine with him.

Reflecting on the case some weeks later Holmes tied up some of the loose ends, for the benefit of my notes, of course. Stapleton had happily agreed with Mrs Lyons to change his identity and move to Devonshire following the suspicious deaths of children at his old school, and he had forced Maria to pose as his sister. Whilst stalking Sir Henry and Dr. Mortimer in London he had locked Maria in the hotel room, but she knew what he was up to. Despite being a virtual prisoner Maria had been brave enough to send the letter of warning to Sir Henry by cutting the words from The Times. She had to disguise her writing but Holmes had sensed the presence of a lady when he smelt jessamine on the letter.

Laura had been the brains behind the scheme using an old myth to manipulate a weak minded criminal into murder and to bring a neurotic old man to his |

death. Holmes had only started to suspect her at her final interview and she might have got away with it, but for jealousy. Jack had shown his true colours when he saw Sir Henry and Maria together, but Laura finally gave her game up when she found out Jack was already married and so chased him over the moor. This led to their deaths but led us to solve the mystery of The Hound of the Baskervilles.

The End

Also from MX Publishing

The Curse of Sherlock Holmes – Dhanil Ali

The acclaimed National Theatre actor Robert Stephens said to the star of Granada TV's Sherlock Holmes; Jeremy Brett; "Do not undertake the role of Sherlock Holmes. He will be your undoing". "You must drop it Mr. Holmes, you really must. It will be your undoing" said Professor James Moriarty upon his first encounter with Sherlock Holmes. Somewhere between the fact and fiction Sir Arthur Conan Doyle's greatest creation stole the soul of Jeremy Brett, the actor who would become the embodiment of the Baker Street sleuth. The Curse of Sherlock Holmes follows Jeremy as he fights for his sanity.... His life. This is the full script of the play by Dhanil Ali.

"I was sceptical when I learned of a play that would tour the north-west in March: "Somewhere between the fact and the fiction Sir Arthur Conan Doyle's greatest creation stole the soul of Jeremy Brett, the actor who would become the embodiment of the Baker Street Sleuth. 'The Curse of Sherlock Holmes' follows Jeremy as he fights for his sanity... his life." I've not seen any reviews, so don't know how it came across in performance, but the script by Dhanil Ali is now available from MX Publishing, and it turns out to be thought-provoking and dramatic, without being unnecessarily sensational"

Roger Johnson, Sherlock Holmes Society of London

Also from MX Publishing

Sherlock Holmes and The Adventure of The Jacobite Rose

Fiona-Jane Brown

Mycroft has a missing agent; the stepdaughter of Lord Wexford Foyle wants a pearl brooch authenticated. Sherlock Holmes has little interest in either until he learns the gem is the Jacobite Rose, a royal treasure. Reading Debrett's Peerage, Holmes discovers Lord Foyle has a brother who is known as a craftsman in gold. Three strange clues - the drawing of a rose, fish scales and a fragment of pine resin - discovered at the last known locus of the missing man begin to link the two cases.

"Shortly before leaving her post as Conan Doyle Projects Officer at Portsmouth last year, Fiona-Jane Brown wrote a Sherlock Holmes play, "The Prima Donna's Last Aria", which was staged as part of the city's "Lost Hour" celebrations, marking the start of British Summer Time. Since her return to Scotland, Dr Brown has written another play, "Sherlock Holmes & the Adventure of the Jacobite Rose", a clever and entertaining drama, ideal for youth groups and schools."

Roger Johnson, Sherlock Holmes Society of London

Also from MX Publishing

MX Publishing is the world's largest specialist Sherlock Holmes publisher, with over a hundred and fifty titles and sixty authors creating the latest in Sherlock Holmes fiction and non-fiction. The collection includes hundreds of novels, short stories and leading non-fiction titles such as the bestselling biography **Benedict Cumberbatch In Transition**. MX Publishing also has one of the largest communities of Holmes fans on Facebook with regular contributions from dozens of authors.

www.facebook.com/BooksSherlockHolmes

www.mxpublishing.com